Prologue.

Dear readers,

Many of you who will read this will probably already know who I am from my previous work that has been published over the years.

I firstly want to say thank you. If it wasn't for your support I would never have been successful as a writer. If you are reading this, I can honestly say I don't know what's happened to me.

I recently received some devastating news. My time on this earth will be shorter than I had intended...however! It has also prompted me to write this. I've already made my wonderful literary agent Sally promise to publish this book for me whether or not I survive to see the finished version. I'm sure Cal will finish it for me if I can't.

So why am I writing this book? It's simple really. I want to tell you my story. Not one I've made up but my very own. About the important things and also it's a story from me to my child who is probably going to grow up without me. I want her to know my story, who I am and know that I'll always be here for her, in spirit if not in life.

I would not change anything that has happened in my life. What would be the point? I may not have ended up where I am now and that would have truly been devastating. I've had a good life, met some wonderful people who have changed my life for the better and I've loved writing my books. My life has been amazing.

So, my dear readers, you may like my story and you may not. But know, that this is me. This is my story to you all and you will know me in a way you never have before.

To my dear husband, I love you now and forever.

To my daughter, I hope this helps you to get to know me a little and know that I love you always. Follow your heart, trust your instincts. Never let anyone tell you you can't do something. I know you can and I will be rooting for you for the entirety of your life.

Julie Thorpe

I hope you enjoy my story.

Love always,

Amber xx

CHAPTER ONE.

This was it!

My big night was nearly here at last!

A few more hours and my book launch would begin. I'd published books before using the indie publishing route but this time, I had a fantastic literary agent called Sally, a great publishing company that were putting their faith in me and my very own book launch party with over two hundred people invited to be there. The advertising for this book was phenomenal so I was feeling very excited. (The book in question was *The Butterfly's Wings* in case you're wondering).

Sally (that wonderful best friend of mine) strolled over to me with a huge smile upon her face.

"Okay Amber, we're all set! How are you feeling?"

I couldn't help but grin cheesily back at her. How was I feeling? Bloody amazing!

"I'm so excited! Literally, I cannot express to you just how excited I am right now Sally. Do you really think tonight will be a success? You think people will buy my books?"

I was nervous. This was my first proper book launch and I was worried that we wouldn't do well. Silly me huh? Sally was nodding her head emphatically at me, the expression on her face making me realise how stupid I was being.

"Oh yes, I think tonight is going to be a massive success! So stop worrying," she told me, "we have got one thousand books here ready to sell and I'm confident that we're going to sell the majority of them."

I gaped at her in shock. How many did she just say?

"One thousand books? Why have we got that many here? There's only two hundred odd people that have been invited. Are you expecting them to go crazy and buy like fifty each?" I laughed, unable to hide my confusion at her bringing so many with us. Had she forgotten how many people we had invited? Was she feeling ambitious about the amount we would sell? I knew that she knew what she was doing, but to me, it didn't make much sense.

Sally just smiled a little knowing smile at me and shrugged her shoulders.

"Well, I do have a surprise for you for later...and before you ask, no I'm not going to tell you what it is otherwise it wouldn't be a surprise now would it?"

"No I guess not," I grumbled back at her. She knew I hated surprises.

"Right," Sally suddenly clapped her hands together, making me pay attention, "we've got a couple of hours until the launch still so why don't you go up to your room and relax for a bit? You're going to need your energy for tonight and I'd like you on top form please!"

I chuckled at her order but turned and headed away all the same.

"Don't get drunk from the mini bar either!" she called to me as I stepped into the elevator.

Me? Get drunk off the minibar? I harrumphed to myself. Who gets drunk off a minibar? The bottles aren't big enough.

*   *   *

Seven o'clock.

My instructions from Sally that morning had been not to go downstairs until half past seven so that the guests she'd invited had a chance to arrive. My nerves were starting to get to me at this point. This event was a big thing for me. I'd never done anything like this before so I wasn't too sure what I should be expecting from it. I did know that it was an extremely important event that would apparently make or break me (as Sally had told me on numerous occasions over the course of that week), so I hoped things would go smoothly. In order to help me get the right 'look', Sally had bought me a beautiful dress to wear. I very rarely wore dresses (still don't) and I would certainly never have spent as much on a dress as Sally had told me she had spent on this one but I had to admit once I put it on that *damn!* I looked pretty fine in it.

It was a vintage style, a bit like what women would have worn in the 1960's where the bodice was flattering and narrow whilst the skirt flared outwards. It accentuated my curves in the right places and hid my knobbly knees to my delight.

I finished the outfit by putting on a pair of white high heeled sandals before I walked over to the mirror on the wall to see the finished creation. The person staring back at me was someone I hadn't seen in a while. Her dark hair was curled into ringlets which framed her pale face just right. Eyeliner and mascara made her eyes stand out, the light glinting into their corners and making them shine bright. The deep red lipstick upon her lips matched the vivid red of the stylish dress that she wore.

I couldn't help but stare at my reflection. I hadn't worn make up or done anything special with my hair in such a long time that I had completely forgotten how different I could look if I made just a small amount of effort. I beamed at the woman reflected back at me.

This woman was a published author.

This woman was accomplished.

This woman was ready to launch her latest novel to a room of strangers whom were gathering below in the great hall of the hotel.

I picked up my mobile phone to see what the time was then sighed to myself in frustration.

Twenty past seven. I know I was nervous but I was also starting to get a bit antsy. All of this waiting around wasn't helping with my nerves. *Ping!* My phone sounded as a text message came through.

'Good luck for tonight! I'm so proud of you!'

I smiled softly at the message that my sister had sent. I quickly typed my response;

'Thanks Ellen! I'm so nervous but totally excited.'

It took a mere few seconds for her to reply.

'Don't be nervous! They will love you and your book xx.'

I was so grateful to have such a wonderfully supportive sister. It was a shame she couldn't be there but she'd needed to work so I understood. She was always there for me. We had to be. We were all that we had left. A feeling of sadness washed over me suddenly. I crossed over to the nightstand next to the bed, gazing down at the photograph that stood upon it. I had placed it there when I'd unpacked last night after arriving here. It was a photograph that I took with me everywhere (still do actually). My parents. They had both passed away before I'd turned thirty years of age due to illness. As I looked at their happy faces, I knew they would have been proud of me, of what I had accomplished so far in my life. I had always wanted to be a writer and they had encouraged me from the start. One summer, my mum had even banned me from reading and writing because I was doing so much and she wanted me to go out and play! She'd wanted me to have friends and a social life as well as doing what I loved which I'd understood. I was only twelve years old at that point so friends were still a big thing for me.

I closed my eyes briefly, trying to imagine their faces as I showed them my published book. I imagined how happy they would be that I had achieved my dream. I was only thirty two at this point, but I already felt so much older than my years.

I opened my eyes, the sadness I was feeling lingering at the knowledge that neither of my parents were there. I shook my head quickly to get a grip of myself. I was still going to make them proud, they would always be with me, watching.

I looked at the clock on my phone again. Seven thirty. Time to go and launch my book.

I placed the phone into my handbag, double-checked that I'd got plenty of spare pens for the signings I was doing and headed downstairs to *my* book launch. Yep, my very first book launch. (Can you tell I'm still as excited about that launch as I was back then? Super proud moment for me). I was so excited that I could hardly breathe.

As I strode into the lobby, I could hear the hum of people chattering in the great hall. This was it. The moment was upon us. I took a deep breath to steady myself, squared my shoulders and walked right on in to the room. The sight that greeted me was nothing short of amazing. There were hundreds of people milling about the space, definitely more than the two hundred that I had thought were going to be in attendance. Hanging down from the ceiling were bright yellow banners advertising my book loudly to anyone who could witness them. At the side of the room was a very long table utterly filled with copies of my book and at the far end of the room, I saw a smaller table with another banner hanging just above it reading *Author Signings.* Everything looked stunning. I was overwhelmed that this had all been done for my book. For *me.*

"Amber! There you are, right on time!" Sally called out as she made her way over to me. When she reached my side, a massive grin threatened to split her face in two.

"What do you think?" she asked, gesturing around the room to the scene that lay before them.

"I'm speechless. Really, I don't know what to say," I told her in awe, "this is utterly incredible! How many people are here?"

Sally waggled her eyebrows at me mischievously.

"Well, I invited twelve hundred people so anything up to that amount. Although, it seems like most of them are here. This room holds one and a half thousand people and it's pretty full."

I just stood there, gaping at her in shock. I couldn't even comprehend how she knew so many people, let alone invite them all to come to the launch.

"How on earth did you find that many people? I mean…how?"

Sally laughed at the expression on my face and the fact my mouth was flapping like a fish during my shock.

"I sent out emails to everyone that I know and looked up people I thought should know you and your work. This," she gestured to the throng of people, "is the result. You already had a small following from your indie published books as you know so some of those readers are here too. Your books are already selling as we speak and your customers are lining up for you to sign your book for them. They can only get a book signed once they've purchased them so take a look at how many you've sold."

I took in the amount of people who were queueing up to see me, a book in each of their hands. There must have been at least fifty people in that line to start with. I was gobsmacked.

"Shall we get cracking?" Sally asked me, taking my arm and steering me over to the signing table whilst I was trying to wrap my head around what was happening. I felt so overwhelmed at that moment, emotions were running through me but gratitude at Sally was the one emotion that stood out. She truly was the best person who could've helped me in my venture.

I smiled in greeting to the people who were waiting to meet me in the queue and took my place in the seat behind the table, picked up a fancy looking gold pen which had been left for me with a pile of extra pens and began.

I greeted each person with a big smile plastered on my face, answered any questions that they had and I personalised each book for them. I wanted to give a personal touch as I always felt it would mean more to the person reading my book that I had taken that extra time to make it truly theirs.

"Can you sign this one to Daphne, this one to Jo and this one to Sarah please?" one lady asked as she placed three books down onto the table for me to sign.

"Of course," I told her, noting her eager face, "which one are you?"

"I'm Daphne!" she told me, immediately carrying on as I started to sign her books, "my friends and I are big fans of your work. The girls were so jealous when I told them I was going to meet you in person! Can I have a photograph with you please to show off when I see them next?"

Daphne peered eagerly down at me, her blonde curly hair falling into her eyes.

"Sure," I smiled at her, motioning for her to come around to my side of the table whilst I finished signing her books. One of the hotel staff members collected her mobile phone from her to be able to take the picture whilst she stood next to me, smoothing down her short blue dress in preparation. I blinked a couple of times when the flash went off, something most phones didn't really do by that point whilst Daphne squealed with joy.

"Ooh thankyou so much Miss Ackles! This is brilliant!"

"You're very welcome, Daphne," I chuckled, "maybe I'll see you and your friends at my next launch."

I went back to signing books for the people who were waiting, chatting to them as I did so. I was pleasantly surprised to discover just how many of these people had read some of my previous work. I'd thought I would be an unknown but it was becoming apparent that I wasn't. It was nine o'clock when my literary agent took a hold of a microphone, shushing everyone as soon as it was turned on.

"Ladies and gentlemen! Thankyou all for being here this evening. I think it's safe to say our lovely author is ecstatic by the turnout that we've had. As you will see for yourselves once you read your purchased books, she is a very talented writer who will be producing stories for many years to come! She's probably got some gems inside of her just crying out to be written," Sally held the audiences' attention easily, "as for tonight, she is going to stop signing books now. Instead, she will come around and mingle with you all. If you've purchased a book that you wanted to be signed but it hasn't been done yet, Amber will be back in here again tomorrow afternoon where she will be doing more sign-ings! For now, I hope you all enjoy the rest of the night!"

A loud cheer erupted in the room as all of the patrons clapped their hands in applause whilst turning to all face me. I could feel my cheeks heating up as I blushed deeply at this attention. I wasn't used to this amount of attention on me at any given time. Don't get me wrong, I felt incredibly proud of myself too but being the centre of attention is something I've never gotten used to.

I decided to sign a few more books as there was still a rather long line of people waiting and I didn't like to let people down or disappoint them. When it got to ten o'clock however, I did stop. I thanked everyone still waiting in line, apologising that I was stopping but hoped they would come back again the next day. After that, I began to make my way around the room, thanking everyone for coming and buying my book. I couldn't stop the smile that was still plastered on my face. I was buzz-ing. This night had been a dream come true for me without a shadow of a doubt. I was finally making it as an established author, still stunned by the success of the evening.

Someone cleared their throat behind me.

I turned to see who it was and I stopped. And stared. I couldn't help myself. The man standing in front of me was absolutely gorgeous. I shook my head, mentally giving myself a slap to bring me back to earth. How rude was I being? I wouldn't have been surprised if I'd started to drool.

"Hi," I muttered awkwardly, offering this sexy man a small smile.

"Hi there," he replied grinning, offering me a glass of prosecco which he had obviously just taken from the waiter for me. (I know, I know. You're probably thinking, why prosecco and not champagne? Well the answer is simple. It was cheaper and for my first book launch, we couldn't afford to splurge on champagne. Sorry all). I accepted the glass that he proffered to me with thanks and took a small sip.

"It's nice to meet you Miss Ackles."

"Oh, please call me Amber. Miss Ackles is so formal," I joked, "and you are?"

"I'm Callum Jacobson, but you can call me Cal," he told me, an impish smile playing upon his lips.

Callum Jacobson. Callum *Jacobson?!* Could he really be who I thought he was? I could see him watching me carefully, probably wondering why I was staring at him. Again.

"Are you the Callum Jacobson who writes murder mysteries and thrillers? The latest book being 'In The Cellar?'"

I held my breath whilst I waited for his answer. If he was who I thought he was, then this man standing before me was none other than my favourite author! I didn't know much about his personal life but my god, could this man write. His face lit up with delighted surprise.

"You've read my books?"

I nodded my head emphatically.

"Yes! Every single one!" I gushed, unable to stop myself, "I love your books! The writing absorbs me instantly every time. You're so good!"

I checked myself. What on earth was I doing? I was babbling like a young schoolgirl who'd just met her celebrity crush. To be honest though, if his books were anything to go by, I guess he *was* my celebrity crush. I glanced at him. What must he have been thinking of me? I rolled my eyes at myself at my lack of self-control. He appeared not to notice that I was making a fool of myself but I could see a glint in his eye that told me he was amused by me.

"Well it's very nice to meet a fan," he said, his voice deepening into a rumbling sound, "especially as I'm a fan of yours too. I've read your indie published books and so, I'm very much looking forward to reading this one."

"You've read my books? Which ones?" I asked curiously. Was he messing with me?

"All of them."

"Right. Sure you have," I uttered, dubious that this particular author had read all of my books. I mean, I wrote romance which isn't something I expected him to read but there he was, nodding his head at me.

"I absolutely have! Admittedly I don't usually go for the Romance genre but yours are witty. They're clever. A friend of mine recommended one of your books to me so to humour them, I read it. I was blown away by how you wrote your story, made it pleasant reading for both women and men so I read some more of your books. Before I knew it, I'd read them all! I'm afraid I'm a definite fan of your work. You had me hook, line and sinker from the get go."

I didn't know what to say to this admission. My favourite writer loved my work? I couldn't believe it. Things like that didn't usually happen, especially not to someone like me. Cal's mobile phone pinged in his pocket, alerting him to a new message arrival. He retrieved his phone out of his pocket and glanced at the message. I saw his mouth turn into a frown.

"I must apologise Miss Ackles. I'm afraid my lift is here so I'm going to have to go," he told me with what appeared to be sadness in his voice, "I would like to speak to you again though. Can I see you tomorrow?"

"Yes, of course. I'm going to be in here again from about 1pm so come and see me at any time. It's been lovely to meet you Mr Jacobson," I told him, meaning every word sincerely.

"I told you, you can call me Cal," he winked at me, "and it's been lovely to meet you too, Amber."

I watched him as he walked away from me, across the room and until he was out of sight. I let out the breath I hadn't realised I'd been holding. Wow, I'd just met my idol and he liked my work! Plus, he had a mighty fine ass to look at whilst he'd walked away.

I wondered to myself if he really would come back to talk to me. It would be great if he did. I'd always wanted to pick his mind on how he came up with the stories he did. I'd also always wondered if he'd ever been a police officer or worked in law to know the things that he knew for his stories. Going by what I'd seen from our meeting tonight, he definitely worked out. The muscles in his arms had been bulging against his suit jacket, pulling the sleeves tight across them.

If he came back, he would certainly be welcome.

CHAPTER TWO.

I awoke, groggily.

I had most definitely drank too much at the book launch the night before. I didn't care though. The hangover was worth it after having such a fantastic success for my very first book launch. I really hoped that I would get the same success with each book that I released in the future.

I rolled over onto my back, my mouth opening into a cavernous yawn whilst I rubbed at my eyes, attempting to wake myself up a bit. I wasn't feeling sick with my hangover but by God, did I feel rough. My throat felt as though I'd swallowed sandpaper it was so dry! I groaned, stretching my arms above my head and pushed my legs and toes out as far as they would go so I could feel the benefit of a full body stretch. (You've got to admit, a full body stretch in the morning is sooo nice isn't it?) I turned onto my side and picked up my mobile phone to see what the time was. The clock on it read 10:05am. Ugh. I'd slept in. I needed to get up but problem was, I had absolutely zero willpower to do so. I let my eyes focus back on the phone that I still held in my hand and noticed that I'd got some messages on there. I had one from my sister, Ellen, asking me how the book launch had gone, two messages from Sally and a final message from one of my friends asking about the book launch. I replied to my sister and to my friend, then pulled up Sally's messages to read.

I've got some pretty exciting news about last night. Come and meet me for breakfast so I can tell you.' I checked the time that she'd sent me that message. 6:15am. Yeah, like I was *ever* going to be awake at that time to meet her for breakfast, had she forgotten who I was? I read the second message.

'You need to get up. Wakey wakey! I have news to tell you so can you please get up and join me for a discussion?' That one had been sent at 9:45am. I scrubbed a hand over my face, rolling onto my back once more as I held the phone in both of my hands so that I could reply to Sally without dropping it on my face (like I'd done many times before).

'Morning Sally! I'm awake now. I'm going to grab a quick shower to make me feel more human then I'll meet you in Costa for a drink if ok? I'll message you when I'm about to come down.'

She pinged back with 'ok' within seconds. With that, I forced myself to roll out of the bed then headed into the shower. Needless to say, twenty minutes later I emerged from the bathroom feeling much more refreshed, (my breath was fresher too thankfully from scrubbing them with my toothbrush) and I set about getting myself dried and dressed. The towel at the hotel was lovely and soft so I spent my time drying myself, loving the feel of it against my cleansed skin. Once I was dry, I picked out a cream V-neck sweater and a pair of jeans, going for a stylish yet casual look this time around. Glancing at my face in the mirror, I decided that some eyeliner and mascara would probably be doing me a favour so I applied that too before starting on the mess that was my hair. Half an hour later, my hair was dried, straightened and looking tidier than it had in a while.

As much as I loved Sally, I was dreading going downstairs to meet her. I knew she would start talking business straightaway about this afternoon's event and the sales from the night before and I was still nursing a headache from that devil prosecco. I wasn't sure I was ready to tackle her bombarding me at that moment, but I knew I had to go. I'd dragged things out long enough already and if I didn't get my backside downstairs soon, I knew she'd come looking for me.

'On my way. See you in a few,' I messaged to her. Sighing to myself, I picked up my handbag, slid my mobile phone inside and left my room. I could see the sky through one of the windows on the far side of the corridor that it was a gloomy day outside, rain pelting hard against the glass of the window. A great day for ducks, for everyone else, it sucked.

Once I was downstairs, I approached the Costa coffee lounge that had been created at one side of the hotel entrance and saw Sally sat at one of the tables next to the window, waiting for me.

I watched as she glanced down at her watch, frowned and then started tapping her fingers on the table top. Uh oh, she was getting impatient. Better make my way over there.

As I entered the coffee lounge, she glanced up and saw me. She motioned for me to go over but I put up my index finger, indicating to her that I was going to get a drink first. I pointed to her in question of whether she wanted one but she shook her head, so I went over to the counter to place my order. Speaking to the bright eyed, energetic server behind the counter, I ordered a large hot chocolate with cream and marshmallows (because why the hell not?) and a ham and cheese toastie as I could feel my tummy growling away at me. A few minutes later, I was given my drink to take to the table whilst my sandwich would be brought over to me once it was toasted and ready. I thanked the server before making my way over to Sally, noting that she'd got a notebook and pen spread out on the table in front of her. I took the seat across from her, setting my drink down as she took a sip from her own iced frappe by the look of it.

"Morning Sally, what's up?" I asked as I took a sip from my hot chocolate. Aah, that was bliss.

"Nothing's up. In fact, I have some very exciting news!" Sally replied, seeming slightly antsy.

I quirked my right eyebrow up in question, a mouthful of marshmallows preventing me from speaking.

"Last night, every single book sold!" she announced, bouncing in her seat in sheer excitement.

I nearly spat out the marshmallows in shock and stared at my agent in disbelief.

"Are you serious?" I gasped, "didn't you say that there were a thousand books there?" I must've heard her wrong right? Nope. I hadn't heard her wrong.

"Yes! One thousand of your books were sold at the book launch last night and we've still got this afternoon's launch to go!"

I shook my head in dumbfounded silence as my sandwich was placed in front of me. We'd sold all of the books? What on earth would we do that afternoon? Panic began to set in.

"What are we going to do this afternoon? If there's no books, how can I launch it?"

Sally put her hands up in the air, silencing me.

"There's no need to worry. Whilst you were having your beauty sleep, I called and arranged for the back-up stock to be brought over. It's in the hall already so we've got books to sell....Although, it does mean that we have to push the official release day in the shops back a couple of days. Obviously, I shall do my best to avoid that but I'm letting you know it's a possibility," she told me gravely. I shrugged.

"That's ok. I don't mind. The book launches are what's going to sell the books anyway. I mean, the people who read these will hopefully recommend it to their friends which in turn will help to sell it. I'm still just in awe that we've sold so many already. How many have we got for today since we're using the back-up stock?" I asked, taking a bite of my toasted sandwich, enjoying the oozy goodness of the cheese melted inside. Mmmm, delicious!

"There are eight hundred copies in there. You'll mostly be signing your books this afternoon, so you'll be able to meet even more of your fans!" Sally laughed, "and by the way, talking of fans, didn't I see you chatting to a certain hot writer last night?"

She waggled her eyebrows conspiratorially, causing me to chuckle at her immaturity. Of *course* she noticed me talking with him. I should've guessed she would spot that.

"Yes," I admitted nonchalantly, "I was talking with Cal Jacobson...and yes, I'm aware that you know he's my favourite writer and that you also noticed how hot he is."

I tried to keep my face deadpan but she was waggling those eyebrows again. I chuckled at her, shaking my head as I kept eating my food.

"Ooh, so it's *Cal* is it?" Sally winked at me.

"Oh, shut up," I laughed at her, "it was nothing like that! He told me he is a fan of my work, I told him I'm a fan of his work and that's all there was to it."

Sally stared at me. She stared for such a long time that I began to think I had something on my face. I grabbed a napkin in preparation, feeling uneasy.

"What?" I demanded eventually, "it's rude to stare you know."

"You said he knows your work and that he's a fan of it?" At the nod of my head, Sally squealed, "oh my god, how awesome! Did you get his number?"

I couldn't even attempt to hide the look of incredulity on my face then.

"Are you joking? No, of course I didn't. The conversation literally only consisted of what I've already told you. There was no flirting, no swapping of numbers. If you're so desperate to see him again, he mentioned that he might be back today. Don't get too excited though, because he might not. He's probably got better things to do," I told her, ignoring the wicked gleam in her eye. But Sally was already shaking her head.

"Don't go thinking so little of yourself!" she scolded, "and I'm not desperate to see him for *me*. I want him to come back for *you*. He was into you, I'm sure of it."

"Mmhmm, if you say so Sal," I muttered absently. I really needed to close this conversation down before she told me all the reasons why he'd be perfect for me and all that nonsense. She really had to stop playing matchmaker for me all of the time.

*　　　　*　　　　*

Half past one.

Only half an hour into this afternoon and I already had a never-ending queue of people waiting for me to sign the books that they'd purchased, holding them eagerly in their hands as they waited their turns to see me. Book after book was placed in front of me so quickly, that I barely had time to lift my head up when a gruff voice spoke.

"Can you make that one out to Cal please, Miss Ackles?"

My breath caught in my throat as I glanced up quickly, making eye contact with the gorgeous man I'd met the night before. I grinned at him openly.

"Hi Cal! You came back!"

He chuckled at the surprised expression I knew was on my face.

"Didn't you think I would? I did say I'd be back because I'd like to speak to you remember?" he said.

"Well, yeah I remember that's what you said," I began, "but I didn't honestly think you meant it. I figured you'd probably have much more important things to be doing."

He glared at me, his gaze so intense and fiery that I had to lower my eyes. I heard him sigh.

"That's too bad that you thought that because here I am. Nothing better to do," he told me softly, "I'm going to head off and mingle for a bit whilst you carry on here but when you're finished, I'd like to speak with you please."

"Ok," I agreed shyly, signing his book quickly as I already should have signed it, "my number is in the book. Call me if you still want to speak if you have to go off anywhere."

Cal hesitated for a moment, looking as though he were unsure of what to say next but instead, he picked up his copy of my book and walked off. I turned my attention back to the next person in the queue who was waiting for me to sign their book.

* * *

Time passed by quickly as the afternoon launch became yet another success.

I couldn't believe just how well we were doing. Sally must have pulled out all the stops to persuade so many people to have come to both events *and* for so many of my books to have sold. I knew she'd said it would be successful but I'd had no comprehension of just how much it really would be!

My hand had even started to cramp from having to sign so many books. I was exhausted by the constant signing, smiling and talking but I wouldn't have changed a thing! I was excited to see that so many people wanted to read my work. This was the stuff that dreams were made of and I certainly wouldn't complain about a little bit of hand cramp.

During the time I'd been signing for people, I'd sneaked a few glances around the room, trying to spot Cal somewhere amongst the people there but I hadn't found him once. I'd decided that he must have left the event which brought on an unfamiliar feeling of disappointment. Silly wasn't it? I chose to ignore it, telling myself that if he'd wanted to stay then he would have and that was that.

When it was nearing four o'clock, I caught Sally waving at me out of the corner of my eye. When I looked up properly at her, I could see she was pointing at her watch, indicating that the event was about to end. I dipped my head in a quick nod to let her know I understood it was time to wrap things up and quickly finished signing the books for the few remaining people in the queue before me. I breathed a sigh of relief as the last person walked away from me, happily chatting to their friend about going home to read my book.

Feeling grateful, I dropped my pen onto the table, next to the pile of pens that had ran out through the signing and stretched my fingers out. Jeez did they ache. It was a good ache though, as it had all been for the people who had blessed me by buying my book. I felt a swell of pride at what I'd accomplished so far.

I stood up stiffly as Sally spoke into a microphone, causing everyone to stop and take note as she thanked them all for coming and showing their support. I smiled at the people nearest to me who turned to clap and applaud me. As they all began to filter out of the room, I strode over to Sally's side where she gave me a beaming smile.

"What an amazing couple of days!" she cheered, pumping her fists in the air in celebration, "these launches have helped smash your novel out of the park and way up into the best seller list!"

"Seriously? The best seller list?" I asked, unable to remain calm anymore. (If I remember rightly, I actually think I jumped for joy at this point folks-but we'll keep that between you and me alright?).

"Oh yes! These events have been absolutely fantastic for you!" Sally cried, flinging her arms around my neck in a tight hug. I laughed heartily, returning the hug happily.

"I couldn't have done it without you though," I told her, pulling back to look at her properly, "you may be my agent for my books and promotion and all that, but I consider you to be a really good friend too. I've been able to count on you to help me, to cheer me up when I was down and to simply be there for me whenever I needed someone. That means a lot to me, Sal."

Her cheeks flamed red in embarrassment. Sally had never been able to take a compliment without feeling like she didn't deserve it. (Which you do Sally! You deserve every compliment!) She gave me another quick hug, then cleared her throat.

"Did I see Callum Jacobson talking to you again earlier?" she asked, all innocence on her face. I rolled my eyes at her. Now she was changing the subject.

"You saw him getting his book signed, yes."

"And he was talking to you, I saw," she continued, oblivious to the fact I didn't want to talk about him, "what happened? What did he say?"

I frowned. I knew she wasn't going to let this drop any time soon.

"I signed his book. Nothing more to tell," I told her, shrugging my shoulders.

This time, Sally frowned. At me. Crossing her arms across her chest as she readied herself to get me to tell her the truth. I'd seen her do this before.

"That's it? You expect me to believe that Callum Jacobson came all the way back to your second event just to have his book signed by you? You know I don't believe you Amber."

"Fine," I muttered, "I gave him my number because he wanted to meet up later and talk. Ok? You happy now?"

She was smiling again at this news whilst attempting to keep a straight face. And failing.

"I knew it! I knew you were holding out on me! Has he messaged you?"

"I don't know Sal, I haven't checked my phone for hours. Been kinda busy remember?" I told her in exasperation. Sally had been eager to get me back on the dating scene for a while so every time a male showed me any interest, she was on it like a dog with a bone, causing me to lose my patience with her on more than one occasion.

"Check your phone then, numpty," she told me eagerly.

I pulled my phone from out of my back pocket of my jeans and glanced down at the screen. There was indeed a message there, the light that alerted me to new messages blinking at me. Sally came to stand by me, shoulder to shoulder as I opened the message up. We both peered down at the words that were written there.

'Fancy dinner tonight? With me? Cal.'

I could feel Sally staring at me as I typed my response.

'Sure. Why not. When?'

Sally gripped my arm tightly as we waited for his reply. We didn't have to wait long before we heard the ping! that signalled the arrival of a new message.

'Great. I'll pick you up at 7pm. That ok?'

'Yeah that's fine. See you at 7pm.'

After I hit send on the phone, I turned to Sally who couldn't stop smiling.

"There, you happy? We're going to have dinner," I asked, secretly glad he'd messaged me.

"Absolutely I'm happy. Now, how's about you help me sort things out in here before you get ready for your dinner date?"

I agreed, glad for something to do to keep my mind off worrying about that night. I hadn't been on a date in years…and I wasn't even sure it *was* a date. He'd only said he wanted to meet me for dinner and earlier it was because he wanted to chat with me. There wasn't much point in getting all worried and worked up over a non-date after all. We were just two writers who were going to meet up and discuss our craft whilst enjoying some good food…right?

I spent the next few hours fantasising about him being more than just an acquaintance. His lips on me, his hands everywhere. I blushed every time I realised how ridiculous my day dreaming was but I couldn't help myself.

When it came to getting ready to meet him, my face was on fire. I needed to get rid of the thoughts that had been seeping through my mind of him. So naturally, I went for a cold shower.

CHAPTER THREE.

I was down in the foyer, waiting for him by five minutes to seven.

I hadn't wanted to appear too eager but I also hated to be late to anything so I'd felt five minutes was enough wiggle room for anything. I was now wearing a pair of green linen trousers with a pale pink blouse. Like I've said before, dresses had never been my thing and I wanted to be comfortable. Besides, I didn't know if this was a date or if it really was just dinner so casual was the best way to go in my opinion. Thinking about it, I didn't know much of anything about Cal other than he wrote fantastic thrillers that kept me enthralled from start to finish. I wasn't going to worry about it too much, if we couldn't think of anything to talk about then our books would be my go to topic for conversation.

The clock chimed seven exactly at the same time Cal came striding through the front doors. Seeing me sat in one of the chairs in the reception, he came over to me smiling a great mega-watt smile at me. His eyes roved over me, taking me in slowly before he met my gaze.

"Hi Amber. How are you doing?" he asked, his voice slightly deeper than I remembered it. Had it been that deep that afternoon? I didn't think so. I replied softly,

"I'm doing good thanks Cal. How's about yourself?"

"I'm considerably better now that I'm talking with you," he gave me that mega-watt smile again, "shall we head off? I've got a taxi outside waiting for us."

He held his arm out for me to take a hold of as I stood up. Taking his proffered arm, he led me outside to where the taxi was sat waiting for us at the curb side. Cal opened the door for me so I climbed in, then once he'd closed the door behind me, he walked around to the other side and slid onto the seat next to me.

"We're ready to go now driver," he instructed the bald man sat in the driver's seat. The bald man grunted an unintelligible response, then pushed his gear stick into first gear and set off. I could only guess that Cal had already instructed the driver as to where we were going because nothing else was said. A few minutes passed in silence and I glanced at the handsome man sat beside me from under my lashes. Should I ask him where we were going? He wasn't looking at me at all, his eyes trained on his view through his window. Had I made the right decision to go to dinner with him? It struck me again that I really didn't know anything about him. What on earth was I getting myself into? I was about to ask Cal where we were going when the driver pulled the taxi over to the side and the ride was over. Well, that had been short and sweet. It couldn't have been any longer than five minutes at most.

Cal thanked the driver, paid him then got out. He came around to my side of the taxi and opened the door for me. I thanked him politely. That's what you should do when someone opens the door for you, right? Although, I wasn't used to men being gentlemanly around me so it was fairly surprising. I looked up at the building we'd stopped in front of. New Orient, read the sign in gold lettering against a black panel backing. The building itself was made of red brick and had a downtrodden feel to it. I looked dubiously at Cal who held the door for me. I walked inside and stopped in my tracks. It was beautiful inside the restaurant. Just a reminder to myself that I shouldn't judge a book by its' cover (pun intended). The walls were a dusky pink shade whilst the drapes at the windows and the lamp shades were all a burgundy red in colour. Candles were lit upon every table next to the flower centrepieces, creating a cosy, romantic ambience to the entire place.

The hostess of the restaurant greeted us warmly. Cal spoke to her quietly, informing her that he'd booked us a table. She slid a finger down her list of names in a book in front of her, then tapped on one, nodding her head as she did so. She showed us to a small table near the back of the room. I sat down, taking in the crisp white tablecloth with the polished silver cutlery on it and the polished wine glass before me. This was a place that clearly took pride in their restaurant. I moved my eyes about the room, taking in the amazing artwork that decorated the walls...there were dragons, Chinese words and landscape paintings dotted all about, giving the whole place an authentic Oriental vibe. I could feel eyes on me. I turned my attention back to the man who'd brought me here and found his intense gaze on me. I stared back at him for a few seconds, waiting for him to break the silence. When he wasn't forthcoming, I cleared my throat to break his concentration on me.

"This is a really beautiful place Cal. I'm guessing you've been here before?"

He linked his fingers together in front of him, resting them upon the table before answering me.

"Yes, but never in the company of a lovely lady," he chuckled as I arched my eyebrow in question at him, "I usually meet my brother here."

"Ah ok. That doesn't sound so cheesy then," I teased him, grateful he hadn't just used a rubbish chat up line on me, "do you or your brother live close by?"

"We both do," he replied casually, "we're kind of flat sharing at the moment."

"Kind of?" I prompted, hoping that he would tell me more. We'd started off on a good topic of conversation so I was glad to find out a little more about him. If he had a brother, did he have a sister? Did they have kids? If so, was he a fun uncle? I had so many questions for him but knew I had to take it slowly. This was dinner after all, not an interrogation.

"Yeah so, thing is we're sharing the same flat but we're hardly ever there at the same time due to our very different lifestyles. I only tend to see him in passing most of the time so obviously, we don't talk too much when we're there. This is our meeting place of sorts. We arrange a night each week to come out for dinner, usually here because it's one of our favourite places and we have a good catch up on what's going on in each other's lives. Plus the food here is *really* nice if you like Chinese food. Although, now I think about it, I probably should've checked you even liked Chinese food..." Cal trailed off, horror washing over his face as he realised his error. I laughed at the look on his face.

"Seriously Cal, you don't need to worry. Chinese food is one of my favourite types of food so it's all good."

The relief was plain on his face but he was saved from having to say anything else just then, because the server came over and took our drinks order. Lager for him, wine for me. Once we'd ordered our drinks and the server left, we returned to our conversation. I was feeling more at ease now so asked the question that had been burning at me all afternoon.

"You know how you said that you wanted to talk to me? Was there anything in particular you wanted to talk to me about or was it just a general thing?" I asked lightly. Noting the blank expression I was now faced with, I continued on, "when you spoke to me both last night and this afternoon, you said you wanted to talk with me so I wondered if you invited me out for dinner because you wanted to talk about something in particular?"

Cal's cheek reddened at that. He lifted his right hand, rubbing the back of his neck. Was he nervous? I watched him as he avoided my gaze. Yep, he was definitely nervous. But why?

"I wanted to have a chat with you because I wanted to get to know you better. You know, find out your likes, your dislikes, how you got into writing and all of it…and I invited you out for the same reason."

It took a moment for what he was implying to register in my mind. I smiled shyly at him.

"So…this is a date?" I asked, wanting to confirm my suspicions.

"Erm…yeah. Yes. If you want it to be that is," he said, hope gleaming in his eyes as he breathed in slowly. I could feel my own cheeks beginning to get hot now.

"Sure. I mean, yeah ok. Why not?" I agreed, "Just let me confirm that you are actually single first? I'm not one of those girls who wants to be a mistress. I don't agree with having affairs."

"Sounds good to me," he answered, smiling again now, "neither do I. I'm a one woman kind of man."

The server came back then with our drinks so I took the chance to quickly look the menu over. The server told us she'd be back in a few minutes to take our order so we took our time, checking to see what we wanted. Over the top of my menu, I could see Cal grinning to himself although he was clearly trying to hide it. I think he was trying to act cool. (Cal, just so you know, you weren't acting cool. You looked like a little kid who'd just been given the biggest ice cream at the shop. It was adorable). I hid my own smile behind my menu until the server came back for our food orders. I had a beef curry with fried rice, Cal had a chicken curry and some chicken balls. (At least we were both going to have bad breath). The server took our menus away and we sat there, watching each other for a few seconds.

"What are you working on now?" I asked Cal, deciding to take charge of the conversation.

"I'm onto the next in my detective series," he replied, his eyes lighting up, "the one about Jimmy Cage and his cases."

That piqued my interest. I loved following Jimmy Cage on all of his adventures. What did it matter that he was a fictional character? I still loved reading about him.

"Ooh, you're doing another one in that series? I'm glad to hear that. I really enjoy that series. Jimmy Cage and all of his adventures...makes me feel like I know him," I gabbled excitedly, then immediately regretted opening my mouth. Why was I blathering like an idiot in front of him? What must he think of me? I felt the blush on my cheeks yet again as I took a sip of my wine to avoid looking at him. Mm, that wine was delicious.

"Amber? Why are you blushing?" Cal asked, amusement evident in his tone. It only served to make me go even redder, causing me to wish the ground would swallow me up. I lifted my head, meeting his gaze directly. I might as well tell him the truth.

"Honestly? I'm embarrassed. You're my favourite author and I think I may be a little bit star struck by you. Hence, sounding like a giddy fool in front of you. I'm sorry," I apologised quietly.

I started fiddling with my thumbs, focusing my attention on them so I couldn't see his reaction. He must be thinking I'm such an idiot.

"I don't think you're making a fool of yourself. In fact, I'm finding it to be quite an ego boost," Cal leaned toward me conspiratorially, "I don't have many diehard fans. It's nice to meet one, especially one that's as beautiful as you."

I burst out laughing at that. Did he actually just say that?

"I'm sorry Cal, but that's a really corny line!" I couldn't help laughing as I spoke. I struggled to compose myself when he began to laugh with me.

"I agree, it is," he acquiesced, "but did it work?"

"Maybe," I replied coyly. After that exchange, any nerves that I'd had about him disappeared. Cal was funny which would always give him extra points as a potential partner. Plus, he'd called me beautiful. I couldn't remember the last time a good looking man had called me that. If he continued like he was, Cal was going to have a very good first date on his hands. We kept talking until our food arrived. Then, for a while, we were quieter as we ate. It didn't take long for our food to be demolished and conversation rose up once more.

"So, have you always lived in London?" I asked him curiously. I couldn't imagine living in a city, much less the capital of the country.

"Yes, with my family. My mum and dad don't live in the centre of London anymore but I still get to them soon enough. Obviously you know I live with my brother."

"What's your brother's name by the way?"

"He's called Ryan," Cal replied, "he's a good lad. Works hard, plays hard, you know how it is."

"Yeah I know what you mean," I told him, "so have you always written books or have you done something else? With your inside knowledge about all the criminal stuff in your books, I've always imagined that maybe you've worked in the police force or in something to do with law. Am I close in any way?"

Cal chuckled at me, his brows rising up in surprise.

"That's what you thought? No, no. Nothing like that I'm afraid. I've been lucky with my life, my parents have always supported my writing. They helped pay my rent until I started making money from my work and I eventually was able to pay them back. In answer to how I know all of the criminal stuff, I've got some good friends who work in the force. They answer any and all questions that I have, helping me to make my stories factual and believable. I'll introduce you to them one day if you like. I'm sure they'd love to meet you," he smiled.

I was enjoying listening to him talk about his life. He became animated as he spoke, fascinating me with his passion for life. He truly appeared to love his life and it seemed he also adapted to new challenges. He told me about one time when he'd gone out with his friends and passed out. His friends had left him where he was and he'd woken up with no idea as to where he was, but instead of getting angry over his friends ditching him, he'd laughed it off and said he was on an adventure. (Personally, I still think his friends were rubbish friends, but I couldn't say anything at the time).

Once, during the course of the evening, I had darted my tongue out to lick my lips to moisten them as they were feeling dry. Cal's eyes had instantly zeroed in on my mouth, desire clouding in his gaze until I'd coughed slightly, reminding him that I could see him staring at me. It didn't seem to faze him though. If anything, he leaned closer to me over the table, regarding me with an unnerving interest. That was when I steered us back to our conversation.

He blinked once. Twice. Then asked questions about me.

"So how long have you been writing?" he asked me.

"A couple of years," I replied, "as you know I started off by self-publishing them and now I've got this book deal going on. There's going to be another two books in this series, minimum."

"What about family? Do you have any siblings?"

"I've got a sister. She's called Ellen. Our parents aren't with us anymore so it's just the two of us now. She's great, a real support when I need one."

Cal froze as he picked up his drink. He placed it back on the table, sympathy passing over his features.

"I'm sorry to hear that about your parents," he muttered softly.

"It's ok. I mean, it's *not* ok but it happened. I don't think it's something to go into when I'm on a first date with someone so that's all you're getting from me right now," I told him, briskly changing the subject to something less painful for me, "I do have a cat though. She's called Minnie and she's my fur baby. Don't worry, I'm not some crazy cat lady before you think I am, but I rescued her from a local rescue centre and she literally follows me everywhere when I'm at home. She's quite the character."

"Well if she belongs to you, then I'm sure she is. I love cats too so

I think if I ever meet your Minnie, I'm sure I'll like her too," he told me, his eyes dancing as he studied me.

Do you know what the best thing about this date was? We were discovering that we had lot of similar interests and hobbies, and if he liked cats then he was going even higher in my estimation of him. The fact that he was hot was not lost to me. It was a rather enjoyable perk to be sat across from this gorgeous hunk of a man who seemed so much like me in the ease that he spoke and the passion he had for life.

We finally finished up in the restaurant, where Cal paid the bill much to my dismay. It was a kind gesture. I knew that traditionally men paid for a first date but I wasn't much for tradition. I didn't want to have him think I wouldn't pay my way. I offered him some money but he told me to put it away, refusing to talk to me until I put it back into my purse. Hey, at least I tried.

We walked out onto the street outside.

"Shall we get a taxi?" Cal asked, obviously still being a gentleman. I shook my head.

"No, there's no need. Considering how close we are to the hotel, we may as well walk back instead of wasting money on a taxi back," I turned towards him, "but you're more than welcome to get one. You still have to get home don't you?"

"Oh no, I'm not letting you walk back to the hotel by yourself at this time of night. I'll walk back with you. Who wouldn't want to walk next to a beauty like you?" he smirked at me.

I snorted a laugh at his words, beginning to walk back towards my hotel. He really was corny with his lines but instead of making me run away from him, I just found them amusing. Cal took his place by my side as we strolled along in amicable silence for all of ten minutes back to the hotel. I felt Cal's fingers brush against mine as we walked. I waited a beat, then he laced his fingers through mine tentatively. I glanced down at our intertwined hands. Back up at Cal. I saw that he was worrying at his bottom lip with his teeth, studying me and my reaction.

"I don't mind you holding my hand, Cal. This is a date, it's allowed."

The relief that flooded his face made me have to bite back my laughter. He was a walking contradiction of confidence and nerves. I guessed he hadn't been on a date in a while either.

"So....this is me," I stated as we reached the hotel. Considering how long it had been since I'd last had a date, I wasn't sure what I was supposed to do next. What the etiquette was. Cal was still holding my hand when he faced me.

"Shall we get a drink at the bar? I know it's starting to get late but even just one drink? I don't want to leave you yet."

I smiled warmly up at him. I didn't want him to leave yet either.

"Sure."

CHAPTER FOUR.

'Bar closed. Apologies for any inconvenience caused.'

That was the sign which greeted us when we went over to the indoor bar of the hotel. I felt my heart sink. Things were not going to plan. Cal turned towards me, his lips puckered into a deep frown.

"Well there goes that plan," he grumbled, annoyance flitting across his features. I agreed, this sucked. I considered my options, say goodnight and go upstairs on my own, or invite him upstairs for a drink and possibly stay over? If the looks he'd been giving me all night were anything to go by, then he definitely wouldn't stay for a drink and just go home. So the real question on my mind was, do I end this now and go to bed or do I invite him up and take a chance on him? Decisions, decisions. (Ok readers, it wasn't a very hard decision to make. Have you *seen* this man? I would be stupid to turn him away). I took a deep breath, squaring my shoulders.

"Would you like to come up to my room? There's a mini bar so I can offer you a drink at least."

I watched as the surprised expression upon his face morphed into a sexy grin. His nostrils flared as his breathing deepened and I saw the desire rise up in his eyes. I'd had a small nagging voice in a corner of my mind telling me that he wouldn't like this forward approach but that voice quieted down when I saw his reaction. I knew in my heart, that this night was going to become much more interesting and soon. His voice was deep again when he replied,

"Yeah. I'd like that. Please, lead the way."

I brushed past him, keeping my gaze trained in front of me as I passed him and headed over towards the elevators. Cal sidled up beside me, waiting patiently with me until the elevator doors opened and we stepped inside. I pushed the button for my floor, then waited as we headed up to level three in silence. Butterflies were flying wildly inside my stomach, batting against me in their eagerness to get out. What was I doing? I'd never slept with a guy on the first date, it made you seem too easy. But here I was, inviting Cal up to my hotel room with no intention of him going home whatsoever. Oh what the hell, it had been *forever* since I'd been with anyone. Maybe if I slept with him tonight, I'd know whether he was truly interested in me or was just after one thing. Might as well enjoy myself in the process right?

The elevator doors opened and we got out. Cal followed me back to my room, still not saying anything. As we reached the door, I pulled my key from out of my handbag and opened the door, just as Cal touched me gently on the arm. I glanced back at him, wondering why he suddenly appeared nervous.

"You know, if you don't want me to come in, then I won't."

Hmm, so he was trying to be a gentleman by making sure I was comfortable with this? That was sweet that he was thinking of me like that.

"No, it's ok," I replied, "you can come in. Although just to be clear, I don't usually do this."

"Do what?" he asked softly, stepping closer to me. He was close enough now that I could feel his breath on my face. My heart sped up in my chest.

"I don't usually invite guys back to my place after the first date. It's not something I normally do."

"Why are you inviting me in now?"

"Good question," I paused, "I've enjoyed your company tonight and as you said outside, I don't want you to leave just yet. The bar was closed downstairs and I have the mini bar in here so we can get a drink. And talk some more."

He brought his hand up and cupped my face gently, rubbing his thumb slowly across my cheek as his eyes searched my face.

"You don't need to be nervous of me. I won't do anything to make you uncomfortable. We will get a drink, chat some more and if you want me to, I'll go home. No pressure. Sound good?" he asked gently.

I nodded my head, still with my cheek in his hand, as I couldn't speak. He was so thoughtful and kind, I couldn't quite believe it. Where had this man been hiding all my life?

I straightened my back, walking inside the room with Cal following closely behind me. I gestured to Cal to have a seat on the small two-seater couch that stood at one side of the room whilst I strode over to the minibar as I pulled the door open to see what was inside.

"What's your poison? I've got wine, whisky and lager in the form of Heineken or Corona, gin, coca cola and lemonade."

"I'll go for a Heineken please. You don't have to worry about a glass, I'll just have it from the bottle."

I pulled out a bottle of Heineken for Cal and a bottle of white wine for myself. I popped the lid off the lager then poured my wine into a small glass that was stood on the counter above the mini bar. Once done, I took our drinks over to the couch where Cal was sat, handed him his drink and then sat down myself. I took a sip of the wine to give me some extra courage now that I had Cal in my hotel room. Cal took a swig of his lager before turning his body to face me properly on the couch.

"Thanks for the beer," he tipped the neck of the bottle towards me in thanks, "but I need to ask…when was the last time you went on a date?"

I almost spat my wine out of my mouth when he asked that. What on earth made him ask that?

"Why are you asking?"

"Because you seem just as nervous as I am and I haven't been on a date in a long time," he replied honestly. I gulped. My nerves must have been more noticeable than I'd thought.

"It's been a while," I replied, deciding to go with the truth, "a few years in fact. You?"

"Yeah it's been a few years for me as well. I wasn't sure how tonight would turn out but I think we're doing pretty well," he said smiling, "don't you think?"

I couldn't help but return his smile. Something about him made me feel so at ease in his company. He moved closer to me, his knee brushing up against mine. He took my wine from out of my hands and put it on the floor before turning back to me. I noticed he'd disposed of his bottle too. My nerves came flooding back full force, my palms sweating as my heart began pounding in my chest. Cal moved his face close to mine, his breath making my skin tingle in anticipation.

"I'm going to kiss you," he whispered, his lips mere inches from my own, "but I'll stop if you tell me not to. Understood?"

I licked my lips. Nodded.

He closed the remaining space between us in an instant, his soft lush lips pressing against mine. I could taste the Chinese food and beer on his mouth, and for some reason, it made me crave his taste even more. He pulled back after a few seconds, watching me to gauge my reaction. I bit my lip, smiling.

"You truly are beautiful," he breathed, tucking a stray strand of my hair behind my ear.

"Kiss me again," I commanded, leaning back in close to him. He placed his hands on the sides of my face, obliging me without question. He crashed his lips onto mine, attempting to be slow and gentle at first, deepening the kiss the longer it continued. I closed my eyes, giving myself over to the kiss wholeheartedly, melting into his arms willingly. It felt as though he were laying claim to me through his lips and boy, those lips were working wonders. I felt his tongue lick across the seam of my mouth, silently asking my permission to enter and surrender into him. I parted my lips, allowing him access. His tongue found mine, tangling around each other as they sparred for dominance. I groaned into his mouth, my desire for him steadily growing with each passing second as he devoured me.

I'd never felt such an attraction to someone like this before. Desire burned through me, consuming my whole being as I kissed him. I ran my fingers through his shaggy brown hair, pulling on it slightly in my fervour. I felt the bristles from his trimmed beard tickling against my chin, turning me on further. I'd been attracted to this man from the start but I found it was growing as he kissed me ardently, lovingly. He was so tender, so reverent in his touch that my heart swelled joyfully. I wanted him. All of him. With every fibre of my being, I wanted this man. I knew it would be reckless, I knew we were rushing things, but by God, I wanted this man. So much that I didn't care about the rest of it. I'd deal with the consequences if it meant I could spend just one night with this sexy beast in front of me.

I caught a hold of his shoulders, pulling his upper body against mine, never breaking this amazing kiss. Cal kissed me harder, hungrier. I returned his hunger as I pushed his jacket from his shoulders. He helped me, shrugging it onto the floor as he kept his ministrations on my lips. I could feel his biceps now through his shirt, bulging tightly against the sleeves dangerously. I pulled back, breaking the kiss as I stared at his muscled body that was so clearly defined through his shirt. How had I not noticed those muscles earlier? That jacket had truly hidden a lot from me. The shirt was taut against his skin, his muscles straining the sleeves to the point that I was afraid they would rip open if he moved.

Cal was panting slightly as he watched me raking him over admiringly.

"Are you alright?" he asked breathily, concern showing on his face. I swallowed. Hard.

"Yeah I'm ok. I hadn't realised you were so muscly," I replied quietly, biting my lip again.

Cal chuckled at that as realisation dawned on him.

"Ohh! You're liking what you see huh?" he asked, flexing his arms to show his huge muscles off more, (even though he looked very comical), "I'll give you a better view."

He winked at me, grinning as he stood up. His fingers moved to the buttons of his shirt, undoing them swiftly until it fell open. He yanked the bottom of his shirt from out of his trousers and tore it off of him in a fluid motion. The view I was greeted with made heat pool low in my abdomen. Jeez, was he trying to give me a heart attack? I felt too hot in my skin, my clothes too tight. His whole torso was toned, muscular, downright sexy. His waist was trim, his trousers hanging low on his hips to reveal the top of the v of his abdomen. I felt sweat trickle down my back. It was suddenly so hot in here.

I drank in the sight of him, unable to stop myself from staring. I could see tattoos on his body. A black scorpion clung to his left arm, bulging with his bicep. A tribal style tattoo laid on his right pec, giving him a very appealing 'bad boy' image. He was starting to look a lot less like the gentleman he'd presented himself to be all evening.

He sat himself back down on the couch, rubbing his hand over his beard. He seemed unsure of something. I touched his arm lightly, a shiver tingling along my spine at the gesture.

"Is everything ok?" I asked him.

"Yeah, I'm fine. I just can't read your expression. I'm not sure if I just messed things up by taking my shirt off, you know, not sure it was the right thing to do," he told me.

"Oh, it was *so* the right thing to do," I said, slapping my hand to my mouth as I realised I'd just said those words out loud. Oops! I needn't have worried. Cal's face broke out into his mega-watt smile at that.

He surged forwards, crushing my body with his as he laid his lips on mine in dominion, pushing me back against the couch until he was leaning over me. I responded, kissing him back hard whilst letting my hands roam over his skin. His left hand moved down to cup my breast through my blouse. I moaned into his mouth as I arched my back, pushing my breast firmer into his touch. He massaged me as he kissed, placing his other hand on my other breast. His lips left mine, kissing a trail down to my neck as his fingers moved to the buttons of my blouse, undoing them slowly. I shuddered as his fingers grazed the soft swell above my right breast. His mouth moved lower, down from my neck until he reached the top of my bra. Slowly, he lowered the bra cup, letting my breast loose from its encasing. His tongue swirled around my nipple, causing my back to arch once more. He gave the same attention to my other breast, making my breath come out in pants as I succumbed to my desire.

I pulled his face back up to mine, pausing as he gazed down at me.

"Are you ready?" he whispered, seeking my permission to take things further.

"Yes," I breathed against his mouth. I'd known I was ready from the second he placed his lips on mine. His lips caressed my mouth as he lifted me from the couch, taking me over to the bed. He placed me down gently, climbing over me as I felt his passion grow.

CHAPTER FIVE.

Light filtered into the room, waking me up from my sleep.

I groaned as I shifted, freezing when I felt an arm around my waist. My naked waist. My eyes sprang open as memories from the night before rushed in, filling me with trepidation. What had I done? I'd given into my desires, that's what. My skin tingled as I remembered everything that had happened, feeling the blush rising on my cheeks. I lay there, not daring to move as he slept beside me. I wondered what would happen now. Would he tell me he'd call me for me to never hear from him again? I wouldn't be surprised, it was the kind of thing I expected. I hadn't had many good experiences with men before so I didn't see why this would be any different. Oh well, we'd had fun. Now I just had to wait for him to wake up so I could get dressed at the very least. Waking up naked next to someone you weren't sure you'd ever see again was nerve wracking. What if he regretted last night? So many questions and doubts were running through my mind that I almost didn't notice Cal stirring.

He grunted then yawned, before tightening his arms around me and snuggling up closer against my back. I felt him press a kiss to my bare shoulder.

"Good morning, beautiful," he muttered into my neck, pressing another kiss there.

"Morning," I replied quietly, remaining turned away from him. I was feeling out of my depth, not sure how I was supposed to act or what I should do.

"Are you going to turn around?" Cal asked softly, sliding his hand along my side smoothly, resting on top of my thigh. I swallowed, rolling onto my other side to face him. He moved his hand from my thigh, bringing it up to cup my cheek in his hand. His thumb rubbed along the line of my jaw, soothing me.

"You're so beautiful," he whispered, gazing at me intently. He brought his lips down onto mine, kissing me tenderly. I hesitated for only a moment before kissing him back. If he wasn't worried about morning breath, I guess I wasn't. I ran my fingers through his hair as our bodies moved closer, skin on skin from top to toe. I felt a certain anatomy of his pressing hard against my thigh, making heat pool low in my abdomen just as it had the night before. My body flooded with desire, my skin coming alive at his touch.

We kissed each other hungrily, the passion rising between us quickly. Cal moved his body over mine, wrapping me tightly against him. After several minutes, we broke apart, panting as we did so. Cal smiled down at me, his eyes crinkling at the corners. He lowered his head and rubbed the tip of his nose against mine in a cute gesture.

"Are you alright?" he whispered in my ear, pressing a gentle kiss to my neck on the soft spot just below my ear. I shivered against him.

"Mmhmm."

"Are you sure? You were very quiet when we woke up," he pressed, his fingers making circles on my skin. I sighed.

"I think I'm nervous again. Silly I know after what we did last night, but in the cold light of day, it's the not knowing what's coming next. I know that sounds pretty stupid," I told him, not wanting to look at him. He took a hold of my chin, lifting my head until I was staring into his eyes.

"It's not stupid at all," he muttered, "I'm scared too. I like you, Amber. I *really* like you. I don't know what will happen next either but I don't regret last night. I'm hoping we can do this again and see where this leads. What do you say?"

"You want to see me again?" I asked, surprised. Maybe he was one of the nice guys after all.

"Yes of course I do. You've got a great personality, you're beautiful and I'd love to discover more about you. You chose to trust in me last night and I don't take that lightly. I wanted you last night, I want you now and I'm certain I'm going to want you again and again."

I gulped at that. Maybe I should give him a chance. I smiled shyly up at him, touching my lips to his once more, letting him know that I wanted him just as much.

He deepened the kiss, thrusting his tongue inside my mouth and taking charge. I traced my fingers down his back, feeling the smooth skin until I reached the top of his buttocks. I took a bum cheek in each hand and squeezed, pulling him closer against me. His kiss grew more urgent, his member pressing against my inner thigh until he positioned himself over me properly.

"Are you ready for me sweetheart?" he asked against my mouth, waiting for my permission to enter.

"I think you're forgetting something," I told him between kisses. He reached his arm over to the nightstand for the condom that was sat there. He tore the foil off with his teeth before moving his hands down and wrapping it over him.

"I'd never forget something that important. Now are you ready for me?" he asked again.

"Yes," I breathed, kissing him urgently, spurring him on as I kneaded his ass.

He surged into me, down to the hilt as I cried out from the sheer pleasure of it. I clung to him tightly as he pulled out gently, thrusting back in again just as hard. He took things slowly this time around (unlike the night before), making love to me as he pushed into me rhythmically. This man was making me feel things I hadn't felt before. I shuddered against him as my orgasm rose up to meet me, crying out when he told me to come. A couple of thrusts later and Cal was roaring along with me.

*   *   *

We hadn't been parted for long before I received a text message from Cal.

'How long until you get home?' he'd written. I smiled to myself that he was checking up on me. When I'd left the hotel, Cal had insisted on coming with me to the train station to make sure that I got there safely. When I'd asked him jokingly if he was making sure that I left London, he'd told me that he'd wanted to spend every last second that I was in London with me. He was full of corny lines but I found it adorable. He'd kissed me passionately before I'd gotten on the train to head home.

'Not long now. Probably about ten minutes until I arrive at the station.'

His response came back within seconds.

'How long will it take you to get home from the station?'

I chuckled, wondering why he wanted to know.

'It's about twenty minutes in a car from the station. Why'd you ask?'

'I want to know how soon I can call you. Promised myself I wouldn't call until you were home but I'm starting to get impatient.'

I stared at those words, not sure what to think. He was that keen to talk to me already? I'd have thought he'd want some time to himself now that I'd left. I had to admit, it made me feel all fuzzy inside to know that he was quite literally waiting for me to get home so that he could call me. I typed a response to him.

'Be patient. Won't be long. I'll send you a message when I'm home.'

I pocketed my phone as I took in the landscape through the window, smiling to myself as the sun hit my face.

*　　　　*　　　　*

I had been home for a couple of days.

Cal had called me each day, sent text messages throughout the days and we were chatting about everything. I'd found out that he liked the same sort of music as I did and he watched almost the same amount of movies as I did too. We hadn't discussed when we were going to see each other next but I didn't mind too much. He was making an effort to stay in touch and get to know me. My stomach somersaulted every time that I saw his name pop up on my phone's screen.

Ding! Ding!

The doorbell rang loudly, jolting me out of my day dreaming over Cal. I went to see who was there as I didn't get many visitors.

"Amber! How are you?" Sally greeted me, flinging her arms around my neck in a tight squeeze. She pulled back then proceeded to walk past me into my house without waiting for an invitation. I rolled my eyes in amusement.

"Come on in why don't you?" I laughed, closing the door behind her. God, love her. She had truly become a good friend over the time we'd been working together, so much so, that she just came into my house and made herself at home just like she was doing now.

I followed her back into my living room, sitting down on the chair opposite the one she'd chosen, watching as she set her handbag down by her side and looked at me expectantly. Had I missed something? I raised an eyebrow at her.

"Sal? Is everything alright?" I asked cautiously, "did I forget something?"

She was fidgeting a lot, looking like she was going to bounce out of her seat if she didn't say whatever it was that was on her mind.

"I have your first cheque with me!" she cried happily, "from the book launch! Both of them were a huge success as you saw for yourself and now I have your first payment to prove it!"

Sally reached into her handbag and pulled out a long white envelope. She sat back up, stretching her arm out to hand me the envelope which I took from her curiously. I hadn't expected Sally to deliver my payments to me, I'd always thought they would be sent through the post to me or I'd have to go and collect them from somewhere. I opened it up, lifting the flap of the envelope and slid the cheque out to see how much I'd earned. I gaped at the number in shock. That couldn't be right...could it? I glanced back at Sally in curiosity, wondering if there'd been some kind of mistake.

"Is this real?" I sputtered disbelievingly.

"Yep. It's real and it's yours," came her reply.

"But...how did we manage it? That's way more than I thought I'd get, especially for the first payment!" I cried, unable to believe it.

"Well, all of your books sold at both of the launches which is more than we'd anticipated and whilst we were selling those, we were busy taking preorders," Sally explained as I listened intently, "I didn't tell you about the pre-orders because we weren't sure how well we would do on those but between the book launches and our online promotions, the pre-orders have gone through the roof! The publishing company are ecstatic by the success you've had so far and we haven't even hit release day yet! So they decided to give you a bonus on top of your earnings to award your hard work. And, we've been able to get more copies of your book printed in time to keep your original release date!"

"Oh wow! That's amazing news, thank you!" I cried, my heart swelling with pride. Sally had done a lot of work promoting my book and I couldn't believe the response it had had. I was so lucky to have such a great team behind me. I was gobsmacked that the company had given me a bonus. It was such a nice thing for them to do. I couldn't stop grinning as I looked at Sally, who was now smirking at me. Uh oh, I'd seen that look before.

"Soooo, how are things with you and Cal?" Sally asked, attempting to look innocent but the smirk on her mouth belied that innocence.

I rolled my eyes at her blatant attempt for gossip. I'd told her about the date and what had transpired at the hotel although I skipped the intimate details because that wasn't for her to know (except now I guess she will know when she reads this haha), and since I'd told her, Sally had been excited for me, questioning me every day if there was anything new to report. Other than our phone calls and our messages, nothing had happened since the time we'd spent at the hotel.

"Things are still much the same Sal," I replied, feeling as though I'd said that too many times in the past few days, "we've spoken on the phone, we've sent each other messages and that's it. Nothing more to report, but it's only been a few days so it's not a big deal."

"The date was last week Amber! Have you even arranged to see him again?" she asked me bluntly. I was starting to get frustrated by the constant questions about Cal. Why was she so interested in my love life? It had been funny to start with but now, she was getting on my nerves. (Sorry Sal, but you were).

"No, not yet."

"Why not?" she demanded, leaning forward in her seat.

"Sally, what is going on? Why are you so interested in me and Cal?" I questioned her, getting very tired of her nosiness. The way she was being was how she acted when she was up to something, which begged the question of what was she up to?

Her eyes widened in mock surprise, her hand fluttering to her chest to emphasise the mock shock as she answered me.

"Whatever do you mean?"

I frowned at her. This was getting ridiculous.

"You never usually show such an interest into my love life. Yes, you do normally encourage me to see guys and I know you were pleased when I went on that date with Cal, but I don't get why you're so curious about when I'm next going to see him. This is totally unlike you and I don't like it," I told her truthfully. There was no point beating around the bush was there?

Sally looked down at her hands, sheepishly which only served to make me more suspicious.

"OK, you're right. I'm acting weird. But before I answer you, can I ask what he's told you?" she asked me, her voice low enough that it was hard to hear her. That's when the penny dropped. I stared at her as the realisation dawned on me like a bucket of cold water being poured over my head. *Of course!* Why hadn't I seen it before? She must have dated him in the past! Now it all made sense why she was so interested in us. Just as that news came to me, I felt my stomach drop to the floor as I was filled with dismay.

"Oh no, why didn't you tell me? You should've said that you two used to be an item! You know I would never have gone near him if I'd known. I'll end things before they go any further otherwise it will just be awkward," I told her, pulling my phone out from my pocket and pulling up Cal's name to give him a call. Sally launched herself at me and knocked the phone out of my hands.

"No! Don't do that! It's not like that!" she cried out. I simply looked at her in confusion. Wasn't that the right thing to do? I didn't get what I was supposed to do.

"So what *is* it like?"

Sally sighed, settling back into her seat more comfortably.

"I think I'm about to ruin a surprise for you but Cal has been in touch with me. He wants to set up another book signing for you."

"He does? Aww, well that's nice of him but it doesn't explain any of what is going on here," I told her, hoping she was going to tell me why she was being so strange.

"I didn't know if he'd told you yet. That's all. I probably should've realised he hadn't but you never know," Sally glanced down at her phone as it pinged to signal a new message, "you know what? Maybe I should go. You can talk to him about it later...Can you see me out?"

I was utterly confused at this point. What the hell was happening here? And since when did she ask me to 'see her out?' I got up from my seat to show her to the door, glad that she was leaving. I didn't know what was going on and I needed her to leave so I could try and figure it out in peace. When we reached the front door, I could see someone standing on the other side through the frosted glass panels. I scrubbed my eyes in frustration, wondering what fresh hell awaited me now. Sally opened the door to greet the stranger.

"Cal! How lovely to see you! Fancy seeing you here," she laughed, turning to me and waggling her eyebrows, "go on in! I'm just leaving."

As Sally stepped to the side to allow Cal access to my house and I took in the vision of the sexy guy I hadn't been able to get out of my head recently, it all clicked in my brain. I turned on Sally.

"Did you arrange this by any chance Sally?"

"Would I do a thing like that?" she asked, all innocence once more, "I'm off! See ya!"

With that, she ran off without waiting for me to say goodbye. So that was why she'd been acting so strangely. She'd organised with Cal to come here. She'd given him my address. I narrowed my eyes at her retreating form. I knew why she'd been like she had.

I turned my attention back to Cal who was now stood in my hallway with me, watching me warily.

"Hi Cal. What are you doing here?"

Cal smiled at me, a little awkward smile that told me he was unsure he'd done the right thing.

"Hi Amber. I'm sorry to turn up like this…I've been speaking with Sally to arrange something. For you," he rubbed the back of his neck nervously, "and she asked me if I'd seen you since our date last week. When I said that we hadn't, she gave me your address and told me to be here today at this time. Once here, she wanted me to message her and let her know before I knocked on the door. I'm guessing by the look on your face right now, you had no idea I was going to be here today did you?"

"No," I replied drily, "she must have forgotten to mention it."

"I can go if you want," Cal said quickly, "I'm sorry for turning up on your doorstep unannounced. I honestly thought you'd know about it."

I shook my head, my shoulders sagging.

"No, it's ok Cal. You might as well stay now that you're here."

Cal looked dubious at what I'd said but stayed where he was whilst I closed the door.

CHAPTER SIX.

I motioned for Cal to take the seat that Sally had previously occupied whilst I took the seat opposite once more. He appeared to be nervous. He was clasping his hands tightly in front of him, so tightly that his knuckles began to turn white.

"I'm sorry if you didn't want me to come here," he began, "I know I probably should have called first to check with you that it was alright but Sally said you'd be happy about it…and I really wanted to see you again."

I raised my hand, attempting to placate him whilst I leaned back in my chair, trying to relax some. Seeing Cal, there in my house, was making my palms sweat and the butterflies I always seemed to get around him were back in my stomach, beating away at their cage. What was it about this man that made me so self-aware each time that I saw him?

I sighed to myself, knowing I should rectify the situation. He thought I didn't want him there but I did. I just needed to explain why I was so annoyed about it.

"I'm sorry that I've given you the impression that I don't want you here. I do, I promise you that I do but I'm also really annoyed with Sally. I've been here with her before you see, where she's given my address out to someone thinking it would be a really good idea, except that it wasn't. The guy she gave my address to last time…let's just say we had to get the police involved so that he would go away," I took a breath as I watched his reaction, "obviously, I don't have a problem with you having my address because otherwise you wouldn't be here but Sally knows not to give my personal information out without my permission. So I'm not annoyed with you, I'm annoyed with her. She knows better. It also explains exactly why she was acting so weird around me before. She knew I'd be pissed off."

"I'm so sorry. I should have asked your permission first too to make sure you were ok with me having your address," Cal said, regret flickering in his eyes. He looked utterly crestfallen. I leaned forwards and took a hold of his hand with my own.

"Cal, it's not your fault. Luckily enough, I'm glad you came. You're certainly a sight for sore eyes," I grinned at him, allowing him to see my gaze roving over his body in appreciation. It took him a few minutes, but soon he was smiling at back at me, a red blush rising up his neck as I studied him. God, this man was gorgeous. He visibly relaxed in front of me as he realised I genuinely wasn't angry with *him*. I guess it was quite sweet that he'd turned up out of the blue to see me.

"Thanks," he chuckled, "I'm glad I can be of service. Although I really *did* come here to tell you something as well as wanting to see you again."

"Oh yeah? And what's that?" I asked, knowing that it must be the book signing that Sally had mentioned to me earlier on. I waited for him to continue, giving him my full attention.

"I hope you don't mind but I've organised a book signing for you on the day that your book releases in the shops. It's going to be held at the Waterstone's store in Piccadilly. I hope that's alright with you?" Cal asked, smiling cautiously as he waited for my response.

I stared at him in amazement. Piccadilly?! Waterstones? That would be a very prestigious spot. I couldn't believe how thoughtful he was.

"You did that…for me?" I gasped.

"Yep, sure did," he replied emphatically, "I pulled a few strings. The manager of that store is a friend of mine from way back when and as they're going to be selling your book in their store, I thought it would be another good boost for you on launch day. Plus, I've finished reading your book and I'm really impressed with it. So, I've been onto my social media sites and encouraged all of my followers to buy themselves a copy of it."

"Really? You've done all of that for me? But…why?"

"Firstly, because I enjoyed your book a lot and I think it will do extremely well. Secondly," he glanced down at his hands, "I was kinda hoping that it would earn me some extra points with you."

I laughed at that. He looked just as nervous as I kept feeling around him. I allowed my eyes to travel over his body again, truly looking at him this time. Now that I was over the initial surprise of seeing him in my home, I could drink him in and appreciate how fine he looked. He was wearing a pair of tight denim jeans and a black top that clung to his body, accentuating his toned body and muscular arms. His scorpion tattoo was peeking out from underneath the edge of his sleeve, enticing me to want to remove his top so that it could be in plain sight. He wore black trainers on his feet which finished off the casual look he was blatantly going for whilst he wore an expensive looking silver watch on his right wrist to finish it off. With all of that and his shaggy hair and his trim beard, he was looking mighty fine.

I licked my lips to moisten them, watching as Cal's eyes fixated on my mouth immediately.

"You didn't need to earn any extra good points you know," I muttered, taking in the sexy vision before me, "but I definitely appreciate you doing all of that for me. I've got to ask, how long are you staying in this particular area for now that you're here?"

I'd meant it innocently enough, but my voice had come out huskier when I'd asked the question. From the way his nostrils flared, Cal liked how my voice sounded.

He smirked at me.

"How long will you let me stay?"

Oh! Be still my beating heart! I knew exactly what this meant, he was asking to stay here with me. I didn't understand why I became such a raging hormonal (horny) woman around him every time. (I promise you folks, I'm not a floozy!). His smile faltered slightly when I didn't answer straight away.

"Ah shit. I'm sorry Amber. I keep being so forward with you all the time that I'm making you uncomfortable. Please don't get the wrong idea, I don't mean to be like this. There's just something about you that makes me lose my head when I see you," he said, tapping his fingers against his knee in agitation.

For some reason, he made me feel guilty for making him feel bad when truthfully, neither of us needed to feel guilty. Of anything. We were two consenting adults making it known to the other that we liked them. We'd already done the deed, we both clearly fancied the pants off each other, so why was I getting so stuck in my head? I kept hesitating, making him think I wasn't willing when in actual fact, I was. I decided it was time for me to take the lead and make it clear to him that yes, I wanted him just as much as he wanted me. I needed to stop being scared of getting hurt. It is a fact of life, when you let someone in there's a chance you'll get hurt but if you don't let them in, then what's the point to life?

I stood, holding out my hand to him.

"Come with me. I'll give you a tour of my tiny little home," I said, waiting for him to grasp my outstretched hand. He stood up, interlacing his fingers through mine and smiled.

"Sure, I'd like that."

I took him through to my kitchen which was adjacent to the living room and gestured for him to have a look inside.

"There's the kitchen," I laughed, "where we've been talking is obviously my living room...this is the hallway."

I led him back into the hallway by the front door, letting him take a quick look around then I headed to the bottom of the stairs at the far end of the hallway.

"Everything else is upstairs," I told him, the huskiness back in my voice.

I watched as his eyes gleamed with hope and he followed behind me whilst we walked up the stairs. The whole way up, all I could think was how he'd got a perfect view of my ass. When we reached the landing at the top of the stairs, we could see a door to our left, two doors along the wall in front of us and a door to our right. I gestured at each door as I explained what they were for and where they led to.

"That door on the left is the spare bedroom. This second door along in front of us is my bedroom, this other door is my study where I do all of my writing and sometimes, reading and this door on the right hand side is the bathroom. I'm afraid that concludes the tour of my home as there's nothing more to show you."

I turned to watch him as he stepped forwards, appearing as though he were deciding where to go. He went to the door that led into my study, pausing when he reached for the handle.

"Do you mind if I go in and have a look?" he turned to question me, waiting for my permission to go inside. I shook my head, gesturing for him to go on in. He pushed the door open and stepped through it. I followed him inside and stood, watching him explore my room.

My study wasn't anything special. It was an old bedroom that I'd converted into my room to write in because the natural light filled it for more hours in the day than any other room in the house. I preferred to work using natural light, it made everything seem less dark. There was a large window on the far side of the room which overlooked my garden and the fields beyond. In the summer, it was a beautiful sight because the trees would all be in flower and the sun always made everything look much nicer. There was a vicarage near to my house and their back garden was an orchard which stretched over a vast amount of land. Their trees always had pink or white flowers on them each year, the petals usually floating down into my garden as the wind carried them away. This was most significantly, the best view from my house without any doubt.

Just below the window sill, my desk stood, the chair behind it facing the window. It was a long desk, filling a third of the wall whilst a bunch of my papers were skewed on top. Bookcases lined the remaining walls, bulging with all of the books I'd liked so much I couldn't bear to part with them and with books I had yet to read. I had one lone shelf on the wall near the door that housed my very own books. The indie published ones and now, my latest one. It always brought a smile to my face when I saw them, proud of my achievements and of how far I'd come.

I followed Cal around the room with my eyes, watching as he investigated my study. He strolled over to the bookcases, tilting his head to get a better look at the titles I had acquired. He grinned when he came across his own books, his chest puffing out slightly as he tried to regain his composure and get his face under control. He shuffled on to check out the rest of the books before turning his attention to my desk. My laptop was sat in the midst of the chaos of the desk, neatly placed in the centre. Cal appeared to be fascinated by all of the things that he saw in that room, finally coming to a stop in front of the window and gazing out at the view.

"Wow, that's an incredible sight to work with right in front of you," he breathed, the admiration in his tone not being lost on me. I went over to stand next to him.

"Yeah it is," I agreed, "when I was deciding which room to make my study, I knew it would be this one purely because of the view. When the sun's out, this whole room lights up and it just feels comfortable in here when I write."

Cal placed his arm around me, pulling me in close, so I leaned against him. He gazed down at me, lifting my chin up with his free hand and searched my eyes with his own.

"Are you happy that I came?"

He spoke softly, pressing a kiss to my forehead before pulling back to look at me.

"Yes," I whispered, loving our close proximity to each other. I could smell his scent, clean and (I think) of Lynx Africa. I breathed him in, enjoying the masculinity that surrounded me. He tilted my chin higher, bringing his soft lips down onto mine tenderly.

I sighed in contentment as I kissed him back. It may have only been a few days, but I'd missed those kisses. The way they made me feel as though I were the only woman in the world. How intense and passionate they were. I groaned into his mouth, unable to stop myself as the kiss deepened, growing more urgent with each second that passed. Cal placed his hands on either side of my face, holding my head still as he slipped his tongue inside my mouth. I had to admit, I enjoyed playing tonsil tennis with him like this.

I clutched at his arms, pulling his body plush against mine. I could feel his hard body pressed against mine and I traced my hands along his muscles in his arms, gently squeezing his biceps. I felt his chest rumble as he chuckled at my obvious enjoyment over those thick arms of his, kissing me harder for a while longer. Eventually, I pushed back from him, breathing hard.

"I think we should take this to the bedroom. Don't you?" I asked, not even recognising my voice as it came out. Woah! Who'd let the seductive voice out of its' cage? Cal fixed me with his heated gaze, nodding once.

"Lead the way lovely lady," he growled.

A shiver ran up my spine in pleasure. (Yes ladies, he growled. And yes, it made me want him so much more). The man was pure sexiness. I led him by the hand out of my study and next door into my bedroom. I mentally thanked myself for tidying my room that morning, as I didn't always do it every day. Turning to face him, I saw him peer around him to see my personal space.

There was a double bed in there with deep red covers (I love red sheets, it's more romantic), a make-up table with a mirror stood in one corner with my hair items on there too. I had a wardrobe, a chest of drawers, a wash basket and a few other bits and pieces dotted around. Cal looked around him for a few more seconds, then turned back to me. The way his eyes were blazing at me with the desire that was heating him up made my mouth run dry.

"You have a lovely room. Thank you for trusting yourself with me."

The next thing I was aware of, Cal had closed the small gap between us, crushing his lips against mine fiercely. His tongue thrust into mine in a quick motion as he claimed my mouth with his, hungrily devouring me.

"God, I missed you," he growled into my mouth, lifting my top off of me and over my head in one smooth action. His lips were back on mine a moment later, his firm hands lifting me up to carry me over to the bed. I giggled as he laid me down, covering my body with his without breaking the kiss. His hands roved over my body, exploring every part of me.

"Can you tell how much I missed you?" he asked gruffly, lifting his head to behold me.

"Maybe a little?" I teased, indicating something small with my thumb and forefinger, giggling at the expression on his face.

"Hmph! Well I think I'm going to have to do something about that then aren't I?" he swooped down to press another lingering toe-tingling kiss on my mouth, "can't have you uncertain about how much I've missed you. Let me show you."

He nuzzled his face into my neck, hungrily. I shrieked, giggling as he did even though it tickled so much that I had to push him away. He caught on quickly that I was ticklish, using it to his advantage as I laughed each time his fingers caught a sensitive area.

"You're not playing fair," I huffed, pretending to sulk at him.

"I guess you'll have to try and find the spot that *I* find ticklish then won't you?" he murmured against my breast, blowing his warm breath over my skin that sent goose pimples prickling along my body.

I yanked his top up to his arms, shifting him until it came off over his head and threw it onto the floor. His shapely torso pressed back into mine before I could appreciate his sculpted body, so I contented myself with feeling every inch of him instead. Cal shucked off his jeans, almost falling off the bed in his eagerness to be rid of them. I held onto him, laughing as he regained his balance and crawled back over me.

"Bit eager there cowboy?" I chortled, seeing the disgruntled look he gave me.

"For you? Always," he vowed, lowering his lips back down to greet mine.

I was still wearing my own jeans, reminded of that fact when Cal hooked his thumbs into my waistband, tugging impatiently on them. I lifted my bottom up, giving him the ability to slide them down and onto the floor next to his own clothes. His lips had barely left mine, unrelenting in their possession of my mouth. I broke free of the kiss, turning my head to the side to be able to kiss along his jaw and down his neck until I reached his broad chest. I pressed gentle kisses over his tattoo, tracing the outline of it as he cupped my breasts in each hand, squeezing and rolling them between his fingers.

I moaned loudly from the sensations that he was arousing in my body, eager for him to take things further. I tugged at his boxers, shoving them down until he sprang free. He grunted, grabbing at my own underwear and tearing them free of my body. I shuddered in anticipation beneath him, waiting as he collected a foil packet from out of his jeans pocket, tearing it open with his teeth as he settled back over me. He placed the condom over himself quickly, placing his arms on either side of my head on the pillow beneath me. He kissed me lasciviously, holding nothing back from me. The desire was coursing through my body as I waited for him.

"Are you ready babe?" he whispered, waiting for me to answer. I smiled to myself. He had asked me that every time so far, making certain that I was ready and willing before he took things the whole way. He was such a thoughtful man, even whilst he was being an animal in the bedroom and it was an endearing quality to have.

"Yes," I told him, holding my breath in anticipation as he steadied himself. He knew I was ready for him, I knew he could feel it. He planted a kiss on my mouth as he surged inside me, pulling out and back in again fast.

He made love to me then, fast and hard, showing me how much he'd missed me. (I have to admit, it was amazing but sadly, over too soon).

As Cal caught his breath, he peered at me from the corner of his eye, running his tongue along his bottom lip. He rolled off of me onto his back, guilt creasing his masculine features.

"I'm sorry Amber. I hadn't realised I'd missed you that much."

"It's ok Cal! Who cares if it didn't last very long? It was intense and it's quite flattering that you couldn't control yourself."

I thought it best to be honest. Yes, I would have liked it to last longer but it was bound to happen at some point. I laid down by his side, curling into him to let him know that I wasn't going to hold it against him.

Cal kissed me gently on my lips once. Twice. On the third time, he didn't leave my lips. Instead, he pulled me on top of him, passion arising once more in my body and, from the feel of him, it was rising in Cal too.

"The first time may not have been great, but I'm definitely going to make it up to you," he insisted, beginning his ministrations of my body all over again.

If this was how things were going to be, I was going to become an

Julie Thorpe

extremely happy woman.

CHAPTER SEVEN.

Cal stayed with me that week.

We made the most of our time together discovering various things about each other (and enjoying plenty of time in the bedroom). Cal had decided that, as I would be going back to London a few days later, it made sense for him to stay with me and accompany me when I went back to the capital city. I'd laughed at his logic, knowing it was simply an excuse to stay with me for longer but I didn't mind. It was nice having him around, plus he could cook. Did I mention that he'd seemed almost too perfect? It was sickening how cute we were being, even I could see that but I wanted to give our fledgling romance a chance and see where it went.

It couldn't hurt to enjoy the perks after all. The man could cook, he could make me laugh, he was great to talk with and I wasn't complaining about his performance in the bedroom. What more could a woman want?

The day of my book release arrived. We travelled via train to the bookstore in Piccadilly, arriving about twenty minutes before the signing was due to start at half past ten in the morning. I was bouncing on the balls of my feet as we walked along the street, unable to contain my excitement at the fact this was my release day.

This was one of my biggest dreams coming true! I'd always wanted to be published properly through an agent and here I was, living that dream. For years, I hadn't believed it would happen and yet, it had. So, release day was here and anybody who wanted to buy my book officially now could!

Cal and I strode through the doors of the bookshop on a busy street in Piccadilly, straight over to one of the employees to discuss what we were supposed to do now that we were there. I noticed a table near the back of the store as I walked inside with piles upon piles of my book stacked all around it. A poster with a picture of my book cover hung above it, stating to anyone that came into the shop that that was the table for signings by the author and it was taking place between half past ten in the morning until half past two in the afternoon.

I turned to Cal with a massive grin on my face, launching my arms around his neck in a tight hug.

"This is so awesome!" I squealed, giddy in my delight at this setup. Cal squeezed my side, laughing at my silliness.

"I take it I did good then?" he asked, talking into my ear before giving my ear lobe a quick nip with his teeth.

"Oh yes," I told him boldly. I walked up to the table that I would be sat at to inspect it whilst we waited for the manager to come and see me. I ran my fingers lightly along the tops of the books, finding it difficult to wrap my head around the success that this book had received so far. The picture of the wings of a blue butterfly were prominent against the white background of the book cover. It was simplistic, yet beautiful, which was exactly what I'd wanted. I could see that the chair that was waiting for me to sit in even had blue butterflies all over its cushion. I thought that was a nice touch. I picked up one of the pens that laid on the table, next to a small box with more pens inside and studied it closely. There were tiny blue butterflies painted along the length of the pen against a white background, just like my book. Intrigued, I took a look inside the box at the other pens and they all had the same design. I was astounded. They were absolutely exquisite and I wasn't sure who I was supposed to thank for this intricate gesture. I turned to glance at Cal, raising my eyebrow in question at him.

"Do you like them? I had those pens made especially for today. I thought to myself, what could I possibly get you for a celebratory present that would be useful? Then I found a place that designs things like that and thought, *that's* the perfect gift for my writer girlfriend. I hope you like the idea."

My gaze softened as I smiled at him. My heart melted a little at the thoughtfulness of the gift. I couldn't help but feel lucky that Cal had come into my life when he did and I was grateful that he wanted to help me in my career.

"Miss Ackles?" a deep male voice sounded behind me.

I turned around to face a man who must have been in his mid-thirties with black hair peppered with grey standing directly in front of me, a warm smile fixed upon his face in greeting. He could only be the manager. He wore pressed trousers, a light blue shirt with a dark blue tie, looking impeccably dressed as he held out his hand and took mine, shaking it firmly.

"It's a pleasure to meet you, Miss Ackles," he said politely, "I am Ted Rendall, the manager of this store. Cal! How good to see you!"

Cal inclined his head towards the man, acknowledging the greeting but not saying a word.

The manager returned his attention to me.

"I hope that you are content with the setup that we've done here for you. Everything is scheduled for the signing to start on time, which leaves us with ten minutes before it begins," Ted Rendall lifted his right arm to check the watch on his wrist, "yes. Ten minutes. Are you ready?".

I nodded my head at him enthusiastically.

"Excellent! Now we just need the customers to arrive."

Just at that precise moment, a couple of people walked through the doors of the store. Admittedly, we didn't know if they were there for the signing or just browsing for new books but the co-incidence of the timing was spot on. Mr Rendall gave me a wink then went off to greet the customers, welcoming them to his store. He seemed friendly to me and I was grateful that he'd allowed us to do this in his shop.

Cal lifted my hand to his mouth, pressing a gentle kiss to it and smiled at me.

"I'm going to stay for the event but I'm going to browse through the books so that you've got the limelight firmly on you. I hope you enjoy it today. This whole event is for you and for you only."

He gave my hand a squeeze before letting go. He walked over to one of the display cases and started to browse through the large collection of books, taking his time to see what was there. I took my place behind the table and sat down upon the chair with the butterfly cushioning. I straightened my back to make myself seem more presentable and picked up one of the intricately decorated butterfly pens to be prepared for my first signing. I smiled to myself as I sat there, thinking to myself how lucky I was that everything was working out the way it was. Life was good.

When half past ten arrived, customers started arriving for the book signing. They bought a copy of my book and queued for me to sign it, which I did whilst taking my time to talk to each person. I discovered I had some fans there too, who had already read my other books. I was discovering that my books were more popular than I'd previously thought.

Even though I was scheduled to be there for four hours, it seemed as though I was constantly meeting new people without any kind of break. I'd thought that it would be slow but steady in the shop, however I was finding it to be just as busy as the previous launches we'd held. It was great to have this much attention for my book, but it was so tiring too.

About an hour before I was supposed to finish, Cal came to my side and whispered in my ear that he'd got to pop out for a while to meet a friend of his. He asked me to give him a call on his phone once I was all done so that he could come back and meet me to take me for a celebratory drink. I agreed to do as he asked before turning back to the next customer waiting patiently for me to sign their book for them. I glanced around a couple of minutes later to find Cal had indeed left the store, so I continued on, thinking no more about it until the end.

An hour later, the signing event came to a close and I dropped my pen on the table, stretching my fingers in an attempt to rid myself of the crampy ache that had taken over the senses in my hand. Ted Rendall came over to me, congratulating me on the success of the signing and to thank me for bringing a large amount of business into his store. He wished me all the luck with my future endeavours, giving me a business card with his phone number and email address on so that I could arrange more signings for my future releases. I thanked him and took the card from him, putting it in my pocket.

I pulled my phone out to call Cal when I noticed I had no signal.

"Typical," I grumbled to myself. As I left the bookshop, I grinned to myself as the sun washed over my face, warming my skin from the chill of the shaded store. I checked my phone again and noticed I now had a bar of signal. I looked about me, just in case I could see Cal walking towards me but he wasn't. I remembered that earlier on that morning we'd passed a little coffee shop on the corner of this street so I headed in that direction and pulled up Cal's number on my phone. I'd tell him to meet me at the coffee shop. I was about to press dial to call him when I glanced up to watch where I was going and stopped dead in my tracks, my phone all but forgotten in my hand.

I could see Cal in the window of the coffee shop, although he couldn't see me at this angle which was good because I was watching him talk to another woman who was sat across from him. That woman's hand was resting on his arm, rubbing it with her thumb in a tender motion. She had pale blonde hair which showed her golden tan off nicely, her body looking trim in what appeared to be a pantsuit. Pfft, who even wore those anymore?

I stepped closer cautiously, trying to stay unnoticed as I took a better look. They appeared to be having an intimate conversation, the woman smiling at Cal when she took a hold of his hand in her own. Cal glanced down at her hand but didn't move it, carrying on with their conversation as though they weren't holding hands.

I didn't know how to react. Cal had told me he was single before we'd started seeing each other, I'd asked him outright on our first date. He'd told me he was single but there he was, holding hands with an unknown blonde woman appearing as though they were an item. I felt an icy sensation prickling over my skin, my heart plummeting down to my feet as I took the scene in. Had I been wrong about him? If I hadn't, then who was this? He'd only got a brother as far as I knew so it wasn't a sibling.

I swallowed hard, forcing myself to calm down as my heart hammered in my chest. I decided I would call him as I'd promised him that I would do and see what his reaction would be. It was my only choice at that time. I pressed dial on the phone I still held in my hand.

I watched as Cal looked down at his phone, excusing himself from the conversation whilst he answered my call, a guilty expression taking place on his features.

"Hey Cal, it's me. Where are you?" I asked, trying to keep my voice light.

"Hi Amber, I'm just at Piccadilly Market. You all finished now?" came his reply.

I narrowed my eyes at him through the window as I spoke. "Yep."

"OK, I'll head back to you now. See you in a few minutes."

I hung up on him without saying anything else. He'd just sat there and lied to me. I watched him rise up from his chair, saying something to the blonde woman before turning to leave. She grabbed a hold of his arm, tugging on it to make him turn back. When he did, she took his face in her hands, crashing her lips against his in a kiss. That was it, I'd seen enough then. I wasn't going to bother to wait for him to come outside to find me standing there and allow him to try and explain himself to me. I was gone in a second, storming off up the street without a backwards glance, hurrying in my attempt to leave before he could spot me. Unfortunately, that plan didn't exactly work out as I hadn't gotten far before I heard Cal shout my name.

I didn't stop. I didn't slow down. I continued to stomp along the path whilst fury raged inside me. How could I have been so stupid? How could I have fallen so hard for such a two-timing liar? I heard him shout my name again, calling for me to stop. I ignored him, carrying on as I was. I heard panting behind me as he ran up and pulled me to a stop by my arm.

"Hey! What's going on? Why didn't you stop when I shouted you?" he demanded, slightly out of breath from running to catch up to me. I glared at him. Was he serious?

"Is that supposed to be a joke?" I snarled, unable to suppress my anger, "I *saw* you at the coffee shop!"

His eyes widened as realisation dawned in him.

"Wh…what did you see?" he stammered.

"Enough," I snapped, "I saw you through the window with some blonde. I couldn't believe my eyes to begin with, I thought maybe it was harmless. You soon proved me wrong though. You lied to me on the phone! That coffee shop is a funny looking marketplace don't you think? And to top it off, I watched as she kissed you! So, I'm done."

I waited, letting the information I'd just told him sink in. I wondered if he would give me any type of explanation of his own accord or if I would have to prompt him. Naturally, it turned out I had to ask for one.

"So who is she?" I demanded, curiosity getting the better of me. The guilt on Cal's face was palpable now as he cast his gaze downwards, shuffling his feet as he did so.

"She's my wife."

I felt as though someone had just slapped me across the face. His *wife?!* Did I hear him right? He was married and that blonde woman was his wife? Horror flowed through me then. I felt sick. He'd turned me into his mistress! I'd clearly told him I was against doing something like that and yet, here we were. Of everything he could have said when I'd asked him who she was, I hadn't expected that answer.

He stepped towards me, reaching out with his hand but I stopped him by raising my own hand, making it impossible for him to get any closer to me without me pushing him away.

"Please, I can explain," he pleaded. I took a step backwards, wanting a larger space between us. I felt winded, as though I'd been punched in the gut.

"No," I told him firmly, "I don't want to hear your excuses. I don't want to see or hear from you again. We're done. I'm done."

I turned on my heel, ignoring the devastation that showed on his face and ran until I could no longer feel his eyes on my back.

CHAPTER EIGHT.

As I got home later that day, I kicked my shoes off my feet as tears finally began to leak their way out of the corners of my eyes. I'd managed to preserve my dignity for the journey back home, but as soon as I'd reached my home, I let them flow. I'd already turned my mobile phone off so that Cal couldn't call or text me. I couldn't face him. I couldn't handle talking to him until my emotions were under control at the very least.

I knew we had only been together for a short time but I'd felt such a connection to him. For him to betray me like that... I hadn't seen it coming. There had been no inkling whatsoever and the hurt I was feeling was tremendous. I knew it would eventually pass but for now I wanted to cry and let my anguish out whilst I was at home where nobody could see me. I hated to cry, especially in front of people. I always went red and splotchy in the face so if I ever cried, absolutely anybody who saw me would always know it without having to ask.

I slipped out of my clothes, yanking a pair of comfy pyjamas on before going to my fridge and pulling out a bottle of chardonnay. I took the bottle and a wine glass with me into my living room, poured it and took a sip. It was almost six in the evening by that time so I wasn't bothered about drinking. I had no plans to go anywhere that evening.

I went over to my dvd collection and looked through it to see what I could watch. I wanted something like a thriller or a horror as I didn't want anything to do with fluffy romances that evening. Eventually, I decided on a psychological thriller about detectives who couldn't find the killer. Until the end obviously. I didn't mind, it kept my mind off of things for a while, my tears finally drying up as I focused on the movie. (The wine helped too).

After the film finished, I flicked through the channels on the television to see if there was anything else I could watch. Unfortunately, my thoughts inadvertently turned back to Cal. I was so angry with him, but I was angry with myself too. I berated myself for not having realised that he was playing me. He'd seemed like the ideal guy...kind, funny, intelligent not to mention sexy. It seemed that he was just a really good liar. There had been no ring upon his finger, he hadn't gone off to make sneaky phone calls and he'd directly told me that he was single. How was I supposed to know he was, in fact, spoken for? I still felt like I'd been taken for a gullible fool. I mean, if I hadn't seen them at the coffee shop, would I have even found out about her? Would he have just kept on lying to me? Who knew?

I sighed sadly. Refilling my glass of wine, I took another long draught of it then picked up my mobile phone. I didn't want to turn it back on but I wasn't going to cook, so that meant I needed to place an order for a takeaway. Maybe a pizza would be good. I wanted comfort food, nothing else was going to cut it. I pressed the button on the side that turned the power back and then sat, waiting for it to come alive again.

Buzz, buzz. Ping! Buzz.

I rolled my eyes in frustration when I saw Cal's name pop up indicating that he'd tried to call me several times, left voicemails and sent me text messages. I deleted them all. As I went into my text message menu, I saw that I'd got a message in there from Sally. I clicked on it to open it and read what she'd sent to me.

"Hey! Firstly, I wanted to say a huge congrats for today! Your first release day has had a lot of attention and I'm so proud of you! Secondly, what the hell is going on with you and Cal? He's called me several times to see if I've heard from you."

Of course he had, I should have thought about the fact that he'd turn to Sally when he couldn't reach me. I pondered what to reply to her for a while before tapping it out.

'Hi Sally, thankyou! I'm so pleased today has gone so well. The book

signing was great too! In regards to Cal and myself, we're over. If he calls you again, kindly tell him to sod off.'

I came out of my messages then and dialled the number for the local pizza place. One spicy chicken pizza with warm chocolate fudge brownie for dessert would be perfect. I placed the order, hung up and noticed a new message from Sally.

'What?! What happened?'

'He's got a wife. Found them together in the coffee shop just by the bookshop. Fuming.'

'Oh no! I'm so sorry Amber! Let me know if you need me xx.'

I smiled at Sally's last message. She knew to leave me alone when I needed it and she knew I'd call her if I needed her. I was glad I had a friend like her in my life. I spotted a small black and white face staring at me through the patio doors in my living room, her mouth opening into a small cry that I couldn't hear through the glass panels. Chuckling, I opened it up and let my cat inside and picked her up.

"Hey you," I mumbled into her fur as I gave her a cuddle, "it's just you and me again now."

My cat continued to stare at me, unblinking. She probably didn't care who was there as long as there was someone to feed her but I knew she missed me whenever I went away. Usually, she would be waiting for me by the front door whenever I arrived home from having gone out but this time, she'd obviously been busy doing something. I sat back down with my wine, choosing another film to watch whilst waiting for the pizza to arrive. My little ball of fur jumped up and settled on my lap, falling asleep within minutes. She always knew how to put a smile on my face.

*   *   *

The pizza had arrived within the hour.

I was sat munching on it when the doorbell rang again. I wondered if it was the delivery driver coming back for something, though what it could be I didn't know.

I opened the door to reveal the man I'd ran from that afternoon. Cal. He raked his hands through his hair as he faced me, uncertain of what I would do I'm sure.

"What do you want?" I asked bluntly.

I didn't see the point in beating around the bush with him. He knew he'd wronged me and that I'd be angry so I let it show.

"I want to talk to you. To explain things," he said, taking a small step forwards.

"No. I'm in the middle of eating my dinner so you can go now."

Cal shook his head, rolling his shoulders as though they ached him.

"I'm not leaving until you've heard what I've got to say," he told me firmly and before I knew what he was doing, he pushed past me into the house and straight into my living room. I closed the door and ran after him.

"What the hell do you think you're doing? You can't just come in here!" I shouted, anger rising at his total lack of disrespect for my feelings. Cal sat down in one of the seats across from the chair where my plate of food was resting. He glanced up at me with a serious expression on his face.

"Like I said, I'm not leaving until I've explained things to you. You can carry on with your food whilst I talk if you like."

I hesitated. Shit! Now what did I do? I decided that it would be better to let him say whatever it was that he wanted to say so that he could leave sooner. I perched myself back on my chair, placing my food plate on the floor.

"I've lost my appetite," I explained as he watched me put it down, "fine. Explain."

Cal clasped his hands together, squaring his shoulders as he faced me. He took a deep breath.

"That woman you saw me with is my wife. She's called Lucy. We are separated," he said, pausing for me to say something. When I didn't, he continued, "we have been separated for quite some time but she's been having a hard time letting go. Whilst we were in the store during your signing, Lucy called me and asked if I could see her about the details of the divorce. As you know, I agreed and met her at the coffee shop. When we were talking, she told me that she didn't want to go through with it. That's when I told her about you. She's quite a volatile person so I had to tell her in the right way. When she kissed me, she did it to try and get me to change my mind about her. It didn't by the way. That was when I walked outside and saw you walking away."

I kept my gaze steady on his face, trying to keep my composure as I processed what he had said.

"We're over Amber. There's nothing between Lucy and me any-more," he said, leaning forwards in his chair.

I mulled this over. They were over? If that was true, it would mean that he hadn't cheated or been seeing someone else behind my back...but it didn't explain why he hadn't told me about her or why he'd lied to me. I crossed my arms in front of my chest.

"You looked very cosy when I saw you together. You know, besides from the kiss. She was holding your hand. Is that normal for a couple going through a divorce?" I asked, silently daring him to contradict me. Even if what he was saying was true, I was still furious.

"No, it's probably not normal," he supplied, "but like I said, she's volatile. You have to do everything gently with her. It's one of the reasons I left the relationship. I couldn't just leave of my own accord without a fear of her doing some damage to herself...but we *are* over. When you left me this afternoon, I had her parents come and pick her up. The divorce should be finalised soon."

I let out a breath that I hadn't realised I'd been holding.

"So, she's ok? How do you know she won't do something if you are still having a divorce?" I asked, hating the fact that I was worried about someone I didn't know but that was who I was. Cal looked me directly in the eye.

"Because she's got a boyfriend," he said softly, "today was just her double-checking that we were definitely over. She told me that she didn't want to give him her heart until she knew there was zero chance of us getting back together. Today, I confirmed that for her. I'm fairly certain she's probably sitting with her boyfriend somewhere right now."

I gaped at him in shock. What was going on here? His wife had a boyfriend but was still trying to get Cal back until he told her there was no chance? It didn't make much sense to me. Cal cleared his throat, not moving his gaze from me as he shuffled to the edge of his seat as he attempted to get closer to me.

"So...you haven't cheated on me?" I asked, wanting to clarify that one thing at least.

"No," Cal promised, shaking his head at me.

"But you spent all that time here with me without telling me you had a wife, regardless of the fact you're separated, and you lied to me when I called you at the coffee shop."

Cal dipped his head, guilt at the forefront of his emotions that I could see.

"Yes."

"Why?" I demanded. I wanted answers.

Cal sighed, scrubbing a hand over his face before he answered me. He seemed worn out.

"I don't know," he admitted eventually, "at first, I didn't tell you about Lucy because I didn't want to scare you off. I mean, admitting to someone you're trying to date that you're married isn't exactly a great way to start things. But then, as we got closer, I kept putting it off because I knew you'd be angry that I hadn't told you about it from the start. When I lied to you on the phone, it was because I didn't want you to know about Lucy yet. I hadn't figured out how to tell you about her. Although it doesn't matter now because that backfired because you saw her. I wanted to tell you, Amber, I really did. I just didn't know how."

"You should've told me from the start, Cal. I know that it's scary to start a relationship with someone new but when you start a relationship with lies between you from the beginning, then that relationship will never last," I wanted to be honest with him.

A small part of me could understand why he hadn't told me on the first date, possibly the second. But every day since? And the fact that he'd lied to me...I just couldn't get past that. It had seemed so easy for him.

"Please, Amber. Can you find it in you to give me another chance? I just didn't know how to tell you...but I would have eventually. I promise I would," he pleaded, a hopeful gleam in his eye now.

I shook my head. I couldn't. I couldn't take him back.

"No, Cal. I'm sorry but I can't. How would I trust you?" I asked him gently.

His shoulders sagged as he realised he'd truly blown it with me. He stood up slowly, his hands falling down to his sides.

"I understand," he muttered, "I know I fucked up Amber. Once you've stopped hurting, maybe you can have another think about it. I don't want to give you up but I know I've hurt you. Please just know that I would do everything in my power to earn your trust back if you gave me one more chance. I hope I'll hear from you."

With that, he walked dejectedly out of the room as I watched his retreating back.

CHAPTER NINE.

Several months passed.

Cal had respected my wishes to stay away as I had requested when he'd tried to contact me again. I'd told him I needed time to myself and I wanted him to stop contacting me. Since then, I hadn't heard from him. As time passed, I chose to concentrate on my work and put Cal from my mind. The sales from my book had done tremendously well and I had basked in the happiness of the success of it, scarcely able to believe how well it had done. People had wanted to read *my* words, words that *I* had written. Even if I never published another book again, I would always be proud of my achievements.

I'd been walking around my local supermarket one day when I spotted a book with Callum Jacobson written as the author. I picked it up and read the blurb on the back, realising that this must be the book that he'd started on when he was at my house. I'd frowned, wondering whether I should buy it or not. Eventually, I'd decided to buy it and read it because even though we weren't together anymore, he was still my favourite author. I'd gone home and devoured the book within a day, unable to put it down. It was an incredibly fast paced thriller that kept you guessing who the bad guy was right up until the end. I may have been mad at him but I still loved his work.

I'd spent a couple of months working on a new story. Following the success of *The Butterfly's Wings*, Sally had managed to get me a book deal with the publishers. This meant I was able to have an advance on my payments and I was secured for a few more books. I'd finished my latest story and sent the finalised version of it over to Sally to get it started in the process of publication and we were gearing up for a new book launch to promote it.

The coming week, I had been invited to attend a Romance

Writers Convention which I had happily accepted. It was something I had always wanted to go to due to the fact it was full of writers whom I admired. It was to be held in London, so I had just finished packing my bag to go when Sally arrived at my door.

I was permitted to take one guest with me and I had chosen for Sally to accompany me. She had been invaluable to me so far in my writing journey and this was a good way to repay her. We'd gotten to talking one day and Sally had told me that she'd wanted to go the convention for quite some time but as it was invite only, she'd never been able to attend before. It was a no-brainer to me, she was going with me as my plus one. It was going to be a week-long event where I would be privileged to meet other authors and listen to various different methods in which other writers dealt with certain aspects of their writing journeys and also, the key note speakers would impart little nuggets of wisdom to the rest of us who would be listening to them enraptured.

"Are you ready?" Sally asked me when I opened the door to her smiling face. I grabbed my bag from beside the door in the hallway and grinned back at her.

"I was born ready," I replied laughing. I had been looking forward to this week away with Sally for the past few weeks, counting down the days by crossing them off on the calendar.

We went out to her car, a little Ford Fiesta in bright green, as Sally had offered to drive us both to the hotel we would be staying in as it had a private carpark. I'd only ever gotten the train to London before because I detested driving there. I could never understand the chaos of it so if Sally wanted to drive, that was fine by me as long as I didn't have to. I'd picked up a share bag of Maltesers for our trip and we ate them as we drove along, the little chocolate balls disappearing long before we arrived in the capital city. We chatted the entire time (that we weren't stuffing our faces with chocolate!), laughing over various things that we spotted along the way.

It wasn't long before we found our hotel and Sally was pulling into the carpark, coming to a stop in a space in the corner. We collected our bags from the trunk of her car before heading into the hotel and checking in at reception. We collected our keys and headed over to the elevators to go up and get situated in our room. I couldn't stop smiling. The coming week was going to be epic and I was (way more than a little bit) excited about it.

"This is so exhilarating!" I giggled, acting like a young girl but I didn't care. Sally agreed with me, laughing along with me.

"It is!" she sang, "I've always wanted to come but nobody ever invited me before."

The elevator doors opened in front of us so we got in and pressed the number for our floor when I turned back at her, staring.

"Are you serious?" I asked her incredulously. When she gave me a blank look at my question, I continued, "you're seriously telling me that nobody else has asked you to go with them to one of these conventions?"

Sally nodded her head slowly.

"Yeah," she replied, "you're the first one of my writers to invite me to tag along."

I shook my head in disbelief. I felt angry on her behalf!

"How ungrateful!" I cried out, "After everything you do to help everybody! Not one of them could include you in this experience?!"

I glared as the elevator doors opened. I knew I was probably being irrational but I couldn't understand how the others that Sally helped couldn't return the favour just once, and take her to the convention that she'd wanted to go to. As we stepped out, I threw an apologetic glance her way and linked my free arm through her free one.

"I'm even *more* glad that I asked you to come with me now. You know that I don't just consider you my agent don't you? You know I consider you a friend?"

We found our room and let ourselves in whilst Sally answered me with a quick pat on my arm.

"Yeah I know you do. No other writer of mine invites me around for girlie movie nights with pizza and wine," she laughed, shutting the door behind her.

"Well you don't *have* to come round you know," I said in mock offense. She started laughing even harder at my silly impression I was pulling of someone being offended.

"I know but where would I get the wine and pizza from?" she chuckled, nudging me with her elbow, "I come round because I consider you my friend too, Amber. I know you're my client but I feel as though I've found a kindred spirit in you. We laugh together, we cry together, we take the mick out of each other. I feel like you're the sister I never had."

I stopped what I was doing and peeked back at her from underneath the hair that had fallen across my face. That had been such a lovely thing for her to say to me. I felt my eyes filling up as emotions filled my throat. Instead of crying, I yanked her toward me and wrapped my arms around her in a tight hug. Stepping back, I smiled warmly at her.

"Thankyou, Sally. Truly," I paused as I watched to see if she could understand the amount of emotion was behind those few words, "right! Shall we get ready and go get registered?"

*   *   *

The first night passed in a blur.

We'd gotten changed into some fresh clothes, other than what we'd travelled in, then we'd headed back down and over to the hotel where the convention was being held at. We were lucky as the hotel for the convention was the next one along on this street. We were as close as we could possibly be without actually staying in the convention hotel. We walked inside to a rather upmarket hotel reception, where the décor was burgundy and cream in its colouring, giving a romantic feel to the place which was convenient considering it was holding the Romance Writers Convention. The furniture appeared immaculate, clean and polished and I felt a fear rise inside me. I'd never been described as elegant or graceful. If anything, I was one of the clumsiest people you could meet! If someone was likely to trip over their own feet then yep, you guessed it, that person would be me! I hoped I wouldn't fall over or do anything to make a fool of myself at this swanky hotel. I was feeling relieved that I'd chosen to wear flat shoes instead of high heels because I would then be much less likely to fall over.

We could see the registration desk over to one side so Sally and I headed over there, bouncing with excitement. We signed ourselves in and grinned at each other. It was official! We were now ready for a fantastic week of books and meeting writers! There was to be a small welcome meeting in the next hour where those of us that had already arrived could go and meet each other. The proper welcome meeting that would open the convention wouldn't be until the next day but this one would give us a taster of what to expect so we headed inside and found a couple of seats near the front. We spoke to a few people who were already inside until the meeting started, then we all fell silent so that we could listen to the speaker.

It lasted for about an hour with each of us receiving a free book as we were the 'early birds' of the convention. Mm, a free romance book? I was enjoying this already and it hadn't even officially opened! As it was still early, Sally and I decided to go and have a meal from a restaurant we found whilst walking around. We were talking and having a nice old time, until Sally brought up the subject of Cal.

"So," she said, eyeing me over her plate of food, "do you think we will run into Cal whilst we're here?"

I shrugged my shoulders, opting not to say anything. Instead, I shovelled some more of my pasta dish into my mouth, preventing me from answering her. Sally tsked at me with her tongue and placed her knife and fork down to give me her proper attention.

"Amber. You do realise that it's a very real possibility that we're going to bump into him at some point don't you? He lives in London," she stated as though I'd forgotten that rather important detail. I sighed, knowing she wouldn't let this drop.

"London is a large city Sal," I told her nonchalantly, "there's a good chance that we *won't* see him too."

"OK, yes. There is a chance that we won't," she acquiesced, "but what if we do? What will you do if you see him?"

I could tell she was getting frustrated at my attitude. What did she expect from me? To profess my undying love for Cal and spend the entire convention hoping I'd see him there? That wasn't going to happen.

"Nothing. OK? I won't do anything," I replied finally, "if I see him and we end up speaking to one another, then we'll speak and carry on our own way. That's it."

I saw Sally's shoulders droop in defeat. She picked her cutlery back up and began to eat her food once more. She was silent for a while so whilst we ate, I contemplated what she'd said. What if I *did* run into him? I wasn't sure how I would react. I hadn't seen or spoken to him in months so would it be awkward or would it be as if we'd stayed in touch? Who knew? A part of me was confident that he would have found someone new by now, but another part of me (an annoying part of me that I wanted to ignore), hoped that he hadn't moved on with someone else. Silly wasn't it? I shook my head to rid myself of those thoughts as they weren't going to do me any good. I could feel Sally watching me, a thoughtful expression on her face.

"What?" I asked gruffly, "do I have something on my face?"

I picked up my napkin and wiped at my mouth just in case I did.

"No, no. You don't have anything on your face," Sally uttered, "I need to tell you something but I'd like it if you didn't get mad."

That caught my attention. Why would I get mad? I narrowed my eyes at her, apprehensive of what she was about to tell me. She visibly swallowed.

"Cal got divorced."

"Right. Why are you telling me?" I asked her lightly, pretending not to care. Which I did. Very much. Sally fidgeted in her seat, trying to get more comfortable.

"He...got in touch with me," she told me slowly, watching my reaction carefully, "he misses you."

I sighed heavily. I knew it, I knew there was a reason why she'd brought him up. I placed my cutlery down onto my plate to give her my full attention.

"Is that right?" I drawled, keeping my face composed. She nodded.

"Yes. He really regrets not telling you that he was married and for lying to you when you called him. He told me the same as he told you...that they were separated and he didn't tell you in case it scared you off and then he didn't tell you because he didn't know how to bring it up. He told me how much he wishes he'd told you from the start. He wants you back."

"Why would I want to get back with him Sal?" I asked her, wishing she would stop interfering in my love life, but she persisted.

"Be honest with me," she said firmly, "you liked him. A lot. You told me that he was basically the perfect man for you, as if you'd written him as a character but he'd appeared to you in the flesh. Right? And as well as I know you by now, I'm willing to bet that you miss him too. You put on a front that you're not bothered and that you don't care what he's doing, but I can see past that. You miss him. I'm right aren't I?"

I jutted my chin out stubbornly, crossing my arms as I sat back in my chair.

"No. He lied to me."

"For God's sake, Amber!" Sally ground out in frustration, a few people from nearby tables glancing our way curiously, "yes! He lied. He lied because he didn't want to scare you off because he wanted to get to know you! He was waiting for the right time to tell you and fucked it up! He knows that. But he's only human, remember. We all screw up from time to time. Now, you need to forgive him because he's actually a really nice guy and he wants you! Don't screw up your chance at true happiness like we read about in the books simply because you're too stubborn to look past your pride!"

"It's not because of my pride!" I protested, annoyed that what she was saying was ringing true in my ears. She scoffed at me.

"Isn't it? You need to think long and hard about this Amber because he won't wait around for you forever. Just forgive him already and see what happens!" she admonished me, making me feel like I was a little girl getting told off at school for something, "come on. Let's go back to the room and have a drink. Tomorrow's going to be a long day."

CHAPTER TEN.

The next morning, we arrived at the conference hotel by 9am, ready for the start of a fantastic week. Sally had eventually apologised for how she'd spoken to me at the restaurant but informed me in no uncertain terms that she still stood by what she'd said. I admitted to her that she'd got me thinking about it so I promised her I would think about what I was going to do either way and then we left things at that.

So, onto the conference...our first day there was *amazing!* I met so many different authors and learned lots of interesting new writing techniques and included in our tickets which we hadn't known about, was a welcome pack to put all other welcome packs to shame! They included a notebook, a pen with the conference details on, a teabag and coffee sachet for those who like a hot cuppa when they are reading, a bag of sweets and two anthology books containing various short romantic stories! I was on cloud nine. It was simply the best gift for us to be given at a conference like that, ensuring that we wanted to go again every year that we could.

When the first day ended, Sally and I went for dinner with a small group of writers from the conference whom we'd befriended as we'd gone around. We'd started talking to one lady, who'd called another friend over who'd then introduced us to someone else to the point that we ended up having quite a friendly little group of about six people with whom to spend our evenings with, outside of the conference. Who better to make friends with than likeminded writers who wanted to discuss romance? We had a great night that night! We were all laughing and joking together as though we'd known each other for years and having a generally really fun night. We drank plenty of wine that night between us as well, getting very merry (and drunk!). Once we all realised how late it had gotten, we decided to call it a night but promised each other to get together again that week.

Sally and I made our way back to the hotel, falling through the door to our room as it opened and we tripped over each other's' feet. Oops! That was when we realised we were more than just a little bit drunk. I stumbled out of my clothes before flopping onto the bed, dreamless sleep engulfing me…

…There was a gentle knocking on our door the following morning. I rubbed at my eyes, groaning to myself as my mind remained foggy from the previous night. I heard Sally mumble something unintelligible into her pillow just before she pulled it over her head, burrowing further into the covers. The knocking at the door sounded again, a bit louder this time around.

I groaned again, forcing myself to roll out of bed and stumble bleary-eyed to the door. I opened it yawning, saying hello through the yawn and not making much sense. I looked to see who was on the other side and paused, unsure what to do next. Cal. Cal was stood, facing me at the entrance to my hotel room, a small smile playing upon his lips.

I stared. Scrubbed at my eyes and stared again. It took a few moments but then it finally registered, that yes, Cal was actually there and it wasn't a figment of my imagination. I frowned.

"What are you doing here?" I asked him, unable to hide my confusion over him being there. His eyes raked slowly down my body before rising up to look me in the eye again. I suddenly realised I wasn't wearing any clothes other than my underwear. My bra and my knickers. Oh dear, this was embarrassing! I remembered throwing my clothes on the floor but not putting anything else on. I shifted uncomfortably, attempting to cover my breasts in my bra by crossing my arms over my chest. Cal cleared his throat to bring my attention back to him, replying to my question finally,

"I'm guessing by the look on your face that you don't remember? You asked me to be here."

"I did?" I asked.

"Yeah, you asked me to come and meet you. You really don't remember?" he questioned me, looking put out at the notion of my being forgetful. I shook my head whilst trying to think back to the night before, trying to remember what had happened. I vaguely recalled finding Cal's name in my phone whilst we were walking back to the hotel and pressing dial once I'd found his number. Oh God! Had I actually called him? Whilst I was drunk?! Realisation washed over me in horrifying clarity.

"Oh jeez! I *did* call you! I'm so sorry Cal! Can you...can you perhaps remind me of what I said? Other than asking to meet you obviously."

I winced to myself that I'd actually had to ask that question. That I was so far gone the night before that I'd forgotten what I'd done. I didn't remember ever having been that drunk before.

"Yeah, I could tell you'd had a few to drink but I honestly hadn't realised you were so bad otherwise I'd have come over here last night to check that you were ok," Cal's lips pulled down into a concerned frown, "I'll meet you downstairs in ten minutes. Then we can talk."

He turned on his heel then, stalking off down the corridor without a backwards glance. I closed the door slowly, panic rising in my body with each passing second. I was trying desperately to remember what I'd said to him to make him come over here at (I glanced at the clock on the wall) 7am?! I sighed in frustration, knowing that the only thing that I could do would be to put some clothes on and go and face him like an adult. I really hoped I hadn't embarrassed myself too much by one, calling him whilst drunk and two, answering the door to him whilst semi naked. I cussed at myself for not realising I'd got no proper clothes on before I'd answered the hotel room door.

Shaking my head, I threw on a pair of jeans and a pale pink top, brushed my hair and brushed my teeth and quickly swabbed some mascara on my eyelashes with my mascara wand. A dash of deodorant later, I was good to go. Luckily, I didn't look as bad as I felt so that was the first good thing to happen that morning. I shook Sally on the shoulder to wake her up briefly to let her know I was heading out for breakfast, then headed downstairs to meet Cal.

As I stepped into the lobby, I saw Cal sitting in one of the chairs that classed as the waiting area, perched patiently for me in his seat. I studied him now, taking him in as I hadn't at the door of my room. He was wearing black trousers with a pale blue shirt, the sleeves turned up to his elbows, the top few buttons of his shirt undone. His hair looked dishevelled as though he'd been raking his hands through it several times, small dark circles shadowed his eyes. He appeared as though he hadn't slept much and a part of me wondered if that was because I'd called him. He wouldn't be happy if it was.

I saw when he noticed my arrival. He stood up from his chair and came over to greet me, then gestured to the small restaurant in the hotel that was open at this time to serve breakfast.

"Shall we get something to eat?"

"Sure," I replied, following him inside when he didn't wait for my answer. I could tell this was going to be a fun morning. Not. Plus I had the hangover from hell throbbing through my head, which partnered with my pounding heart, was not a good mixture. Maybe with something non-alcoholic to drink and some food down me, I might start to feel better...and having this chat with Cal was probably a good idea. I'd be able to either sort things out with him or end them but either way I'd have answers. I swallowed hard, knowing this could be an intense few minutes. We were seated by the host at a small table near the back of the restaurant. There was nobody else near us to hear anything we said.

"Can I get you any drinks?" the waitress asked us as she came over with a bright smile planted firmly on her face.

"Yes, thank you. I'll have a coffee and she'll have a hot chocolate please. That's all for the moment," Cal told the young woman, looking at me directly as he ordered. I sniffed in annoyance.

"How did you know I would want a hot chocolate instead of something else?"

Cal never broke his gaze from mine as he answered my question with ease.

"Because I remember. From before. You don't like tea or coffee but you do like hot chocolate. You don't like anything else to drink on the morning after a drinking session because a hot chocolate makes you feel better every time."

I slumped back in my seat, surprised that he remembered that detail. I appraised him with different eyes. If he could remember something that small after such a short time together, he'd paid more attention that I'd given him credit for. Maybe we could work after all.

"Thank you," I said, my voice hoarse, "soooo....do you care to enlighten me on our conversation from last night?"

Cal leaned forwards in his chair, bridging his hands together in front of his face.

"You asked me to come over this morning, and at this time so that one's on you, so that we could talk. About us. You told me that you wanted to try again and that you've forgiven me for my sins."

I closed my eyes in relief. I hadn't been stupid or embarrassing after all, I'd just been honest with him. With myself. Thank the Lord. However, Cal decided to continue speaking.

"You did kinda go on to tell me how much you've missed me and my muscular arms and my tight ass, I think that's what you said. It was then I'd realised you were drunk. Up until that point, you'd been talking normally without any indication that you were hammered."

I cringed to hear that. So I *had* made a fool of myself then. What an idiot I was.

"I'm sorry for calling you when I was drunk. It's not something I ever usually do."

Cal relaxed slightly at my disclosure, sitting back as our drinks were delivered to our table. I took a much needed sip of my hot chocolate whilst I pondered on what was going to happen next.

"How's your drink?" Cal asked me as he sipped on his coffee.

"It's nice, thankyou. What…erm…what happens now?" I asked shyly.

"That depends," came the husky voiced reply, "I know that you were drunk last night when you called so I don't know if you meant what you said about wanting to try things again with me. I guess, I just need to know, did you mean it? Do you want me?"

I took in a deep breath at the brutally honest speech. It was now or never. I met his gaze evenly, hearing Sally's voice ringing in my ears telling me to sort myself out and give him a chance.

"Cal? I'll be honest. Sally gave me a good talking to the other night. She told me that you'd been in touch with her and told her that you missed me. Is that true?"

Cal nodded his head, not saying a word, allowing me to finish.

"OK. So, if I'm honest, I've missed you too," I admitted to him, glancing down at my drink to avoid his acute gaze briefly, "and Sally made me realise that even though you hurt me, I needed to forgive you. You made a mistake. One that you regret…she also made me realise that if I ever want to be happy, then I needed to make amends with you. You are my chance at true happiness. I know that sounds sappy and clichéd but it's the truth. So if you truly want to try again at our relationship, then I'm willing to try as well."

Cal smiled brightly at me, his whole face lighting up as though a burden had just been lifted from his shoulders.

"You are?" he asked, as though he didn't quite believe it.

"Yes. On one condition," I said firmly, "that this time around, we don't keep secrets from each other. If I find out that you've kept secrets from me or lie to me again, then I will leave and not give you any more chances. Understood?"

"Absolutely. I can agree to that and I can promise you that I won't ever hurt you like that again," he told me earnestly. He reached across the table, folding his hand over mine, rubbing his thumb lightly across my knuckles in a loving gesture.

"OK then," then to try and lighten things up a bit, "so what's new with you? I saw you released a new book. It was really good by the way."

We spent the rest of our time at breakfast catching up on all of the things we'd both been up to whilst we'd been apart. Cal finally told me all about the ex-wife and what had happened there. They'd gotten married when they were young, only to grow apart as they grew older, realising that they weren't compatible after all. They'd wanted different things so they'd finally said goodbye so that they could move on with their lives.

Once we had finally had that conversation and cleared the air, things started to feel much better between us. It turned out that all we'd needed to do was talk things through properly without me being stubborn and refusing to sort things out. I was beginning to feel as though we maybe *could* have a future together. I was going to go into it with my eyes wide open and no secrets. Hopefully.

CHAPTER ELEVEN.

After I'd received a call from Sally a while later, Cal and I had said our goodbyes so that I could meet Sally and head over to the conference. Cal and I arranged to meet again a few days later for dinner so that I could enjoy the rest of my time with Sally at the conference which I did. We spent the rest of our time there visiting with new and current authors who all happily gave me their advice for various parts of writing a book and marketing. Even though I had been a relatively successful writer up until that point, there was still a large amount of information that I hadn't previously known. It was almost overwhelming to think how much I had been skating by in my career that I felt slightly ashamed.

Sally attempted to make me feel better about it by telling me that we were doing all of the right things now and that was all that mattered. To her credit, it did cheer me up a bit but Sally had a knack for being able to do that whilst appearing incredibly sincere about what she said (even when it wasn't true).

We both went out with the same group of women that we had on the first night a couple of times but none of us drank anywhere near as much as we had previously. It turned out that Sally and I weren't the only ones nursing awful hangovers the next morning which I personally was glad to hear about.

As the conference came to an end, Sally and I walked back to the hotel, discussing animatedly about the things we had seen and learned over the past week. It had been fantastic, truly opening my eyes to interesting new angles and ways to deal with problems that arose. Once we stepped inside our room, Sally turned to me in a swift fluid motion, causing me to squawk in surprise by the suddenness of it.

"I've got to tell you something," she stated.

"What?" I asked, preparing myself for something unpleasant to come my way.

"Don't look so worried!" she laughed, "It's nothing bad! I know you're meeting Cal tonight for a meal and to start dating again, which I approve of one hundred percent by the way, so I'm going to head home tonight and leave you to have this room for the last night we'd booked on your own. You know, so you can bring a certain someone back after your date without worrying about me being here and preventing you from getting down and dirty with him."

She waggled her eyebrows at me mischievously as I rolled my eyes, laughing along with her now.

"As if you just said that!" I howled, letting my laughter take over at the fact that she had just told me I had a night in the hotel without her to bring my boyfriend home and well, you can imagine the rest.

"What? I only speak the truth," Sally chuckled, shrugging her shoulders at me, "you telling me that's not precisely what's going to happen?"

"Well, it's not something I was planning to tell you!"

She continued laughing as she picked up her bag from the floor which she had already packed by the looks of it.

"Aw, come on Amber! I'm a grown up woman who has read your books! There is no way that you can convince me that's not on your mind. So I'm heading off now to get out of your hair. Cal has said he'll drive you home tomorrow so I think it's safe to say, you're good to go!"

Sally came over to give me a quick hug before she left, clicking the door shut quietly behind her as I sat down on my bed, my thoughts racing wildly at what was to come. I couldn't believe she'd done that for me, even though as I thought about it, I *could* believe it. She was an extraordinarily kind person whom I was grateful to call my friend.

I glanced at the time, slightly alarmed to see just how late in the day it was. Cal would be there soon and I still needed to get ready! Searching through my clothes that I'd taken with me on that trip, I decided to go with a low cut red top, a tight pair of jeans and my black high heeled boots that I'd carried along just in case I'd need them for anything. Good thing I had right? I brushed my hair so that it appeared to be tamed (even though it probably wouldn't last long) and topped up the make up on my face, finishing just in time for Cal to arrive at my door.

I opened it up and greeted him with a smile, noticing that he'd got flowers in his hand.

"These are for you," he grinned at me, holding the flowers out to me. They were beautiful, all various vivid colours that brightened up the room in an instant. What a lovely gift, I thought to myself.

"Thankyou, they're gorgeous," I told him, taking them and turning to place them on the stand near the door for when I returned later that night before closing the door to head out with him.

*   *   *

Cal had taken me to a local Italian place, deciding a hearty pasta dish would be great food for our reconciliation. As he put it, we needed the comfort food so we might as well just enjoy it. He didn't need to tell me twice, I'll tell you. I ordered a spaghetti Bolognese with parmesan cheese, regretting my choice as soon as I started to eat it. It wasn't that the meal was horrible or anything along those lines, but it reminded me of why I never usually ate spaghetti in public. I made a mess. It was that simple. I was attempting to twist the pasta around the prongs of my fork when I accidentally flicked Bolognese sauce across the table, I dropped the spaghetti plenty of times and generally found it difficult to eat.

Cal had chuckled at my frustration as I grimaced at the ordeal I was undertaking just to eat my dinner and told me not to worry about it. I'd rolled my eyes at that then because that was such a typical guy answer if ever there was one.

When we'd finally finished our meals, we headed back towards the hotel whilst I thanked God that it was over. (Honestly readers, you've no idea just how much I hated that meal. I haven't eaten spaghetti since either by the way). Cal had insisted on walking me back to make sure I got there safely. I'd kept the fact that Sally had already left a secret through the meal as I'd wanted to see how the evening would go first. Fortunately, Sally had been right of course. It had gone rather well and my heart was already starting to pound in anticipation of me asking him to go upstairs with me. Even though he'd known my body before, I was apprehensive about what he would think of me now. I know I shouldn't have worried, but hey, I'm a woman and it was something that mattered to me.

We came to a stop outside of my hotel, our fingers tangled together as Cal held onto me, a wistful look upon his face.

"It's a shame Sally's up there. I would have loved to spend the rest of the night with you," Cal murmured, pulling me in close so he could rest his chin upon my head. I smiled, closing my eyes as I leaned into him.

"That's good to know, considering she's gone home."

Cal stepped backwards, his eyes widening at me in surprise.

"What?" he spluttered. I grinned wickedly up at him as I replied,

"She's gone home. So if you'd like to come upstairs and spend the rest of the night with me, then you're more than welcome to."

"Is that why she asked me to take you home tomorrow then? She told me that she was having car trouble! I'd assumed I'd be taking the both of you home," Cal told me, working things out quickly in his head. I shrugged my shoulders at him.

"I've no idea what she told you Cal so I can't give an explanation for her actions but she's gone and she told me that you would be taking me home. So, what do you say? Want to come up and get truly reacquainted with each other?" I asked him coyly. I'd already decided that there was no point in beating around the bush with him anymore.

Cal grinned at the invitation, gesturing for me to lead the way. We went inside and up to my hotel room, mere minutes passing by but the atmosphere between us was heating up fast. As soon as we were through the door, Cal kissed me hard on my mouth, pushing me up against the now closed door whilst pinning my hands above my head. I arched my body into his, moaning into the kiss as desire raced through my veins. God, I had missed this. The memory of his kisses had faded from my memory for a while but it all came back full force at that moment. This man practically exuded passion and sex.

Cal deepened the kiss, thrusting his tongue into my mouth as he reached down to grasp my breast in his hand, allowing my arm to move. I stroked my fingers through his hair, loving the feel of it running underneath my touch as he broke the kiss to take things over to the bed. Before we climbed onto it, we tore our clothes off of each other in quick, almost frantic movements. I couldn't get enough of him and from how he was being, I could tell that Cal couldn't get enough of me either.

Once our clothes were on the floor and nothing stood in our way, we fell onto the bed in each other's arms, our lips colliding together as our passion grew to supernova levels. I rolled us over so that I was on top, tracing a line of kisses down his chest, taking my time to show every inch of his body my appreciation for it. His hands curled around me. He pulled me up to him, turning us so that he was back on top of me. I could feel him pushing against my inner thigh, his hardness evident in his excitement. I rubbed my body against his, spurring him on to plunge deep into my core, a growl escaping his lips as the pleasure hit us both intensely.

"I've missed you so much," he grunted into my ear as he thrust into me over and over, his pace picking up speed with each one.

I wrapped my arms around his toned torso, pressing my lips into his biceps and kissing along the lines of his tattoos. I held on for dear life as pleasure rocked my body, crying out mere moments before Cal did, our panting breaths all that could be heard between us for several minutes.

After a short time, Cal lifted his head to peer into my face and pressed a gentle kiss against my lips. He rolled off of my body and laid down by my side, resting his arm around my shoulders to allow me to snuggle up into him. I sighed in contentment to myself. This was just what I needed right then. To be in the knowledge that there was someone out there who wanted me and who hadn't given up on me whilst I found my way back to them. A smile played upon my lips as I fell asleep next to him, dreaming of the wonderful things that were yet to come.

CHAPTER TWELVE.

Cal had driven me home the next day, staying with me for the weekend so that we could enjoy some extra time together before he had to leave on the Sunday evening. He'd got a meeting with his publisher on the Monday morning so he'd got to get back. I didn't mind too much that he was going home for a few days, I was absolutely exhausted from all of the love making we'd done over the course of the weekend. Not that I was complaining of course, I'd been abstinent for months in between my time dating Cal but a couple of days reprieve would probably do us both good at that point.

On the Monday morning, I'd called Sally to have a proper catch up about things since I'd seen her. I'd sent her a message to say thankyou for what she'd done and to let her know I'd gotten home the next morning but the phone call was the first time I'd properly spoken to her. Naturally, she'd wanted to know all of the gossip so I told her the majority of what had happened and when she asked, I confirmed that yes, Cal and myself were definitely a couple and that we were going to see what happened for us. Sally had squealed down the phone at me, causing me to take it away from my ear so that I didn't go deaf, but I couldn't help being amused by her happiness over it.

After we'd caught up on the weekend, Sally and I discussed the conference and what we'd learned whilst we were there. There had been so much knowledge and so many tips imparted to us that we knew we had to give a few of those things a try. We agreed to try some of the new marketing ideas for my latest book, our hard work eventually paying off when the book became a best seller within the first two weeks of its' release. It proved to be more of a success than my first book with this particular publishing company, 'The Butterfly's Wings,' which I was completely gobsmacked by. I'd never thought in a million years that my books would become bestsellers! Cal remained by my side throughout the whole of that time, our relationship growing ever stronger all the time. He supported my journey in my writing career as I supported his.

Months passed.

We'd been together for several months when I asked Cal to move in with me. It had made sense for him to move into my house as I already owned it and he had been sharing a flat with his brother. I know some people might think that moving in together that fast was a bad idea, but it wasn't to us. It made perfect sense. We were happy, we were serious about each other and as he was already around at my house most of the time, I decided I might as well ask. And yes, he agreed to move in and share my life fully with me. Why wouldn't he? Haha!

A few more months passed and I knew, in my bones, that I'd found my ideal man. We never argued, we got on well together and the sex was incredible! We decided to spend our next Christmas together with our families, all in one place. That meant that Cal's parents, his brother, Cal and myself and my sister would all be there. Cal's parents had invited us around to theirs so that they could host and I had to admit, I was really looking forward to being at a proper family Christmas with my sister as we hadn't had one with a bunch of family members around for a long time. I'd met Cal's parents several times by then and I liked them tremendously. They always made me feel welcome and seemed interested in my life which was nice. They were extremely kind and reminded me of my own parents.

My sister, Ellen, would be joining us for Christmas but her husband had to work away so he wouldn't be joining us. I was a little bit glad that he wasn't going because I wasn't a massive fan of his. I simply tolerated him for Ellen's sake. I didn't know what it was about him, but something seemed off with him.

Cal's parents lived just outside of London these days in the Hemel Hempstead area and their house was simply beautiful.

It held a large gravel driveway with tall green willow trees on either side which gave it a magical feel to it as you drove in. When you looked upon the house itself, it was enormous yet beautiful. Pretty flowers hung by the doors in hanging baskets whilst the white windowsill panes made the red of the brick truly stand out. I always felt a sense of happiness when I saw that house, as though I were stepping into another world.

We drove over to their house on Christmas Eve, arriving just after two in the afternoon. Ellen had come with us in our car as we'd realised it would be silly to take two cars when she lived close by to me and we were heading in the same direction. After we'd knocked on the door, we were greeted by Cal's parents, Harry and Rachel. Rachel gave me a tight hug before releasing me and smiling warmly at us all.

"Hello! It's so good to see you all," she greeted us as Harry gave me a quick peck on my cheek in welcome, "come on, come in! It's cold out here, we don't want any of you catching a cold now do we?"

Cal, Ellen and myself stepped into the lovely house and followed the older man and woman through the hallway by the front door, into the living room. As I walked through into the room, I noticed someone already in there, lounging on the sofa languidly until he saw us, at which point he jumped up and pulled us into a hug (except Ellen because he hadn't met her yet). It was Cal's brother, grinning at us like a Cheshire cat as he stepped back from us.

"Cal! Amber! It's great to see you! And I'm guessing this is Ellen?" he asked curiously. As they were finally meeting each other for the first time, I decided to introduce them.

"Yep, this is my sister, Ellen. Ellen, this is Cal's brother, Ryan."

They said hello to each other with small, awkward smiles. I knew they'd only just met but I had a good feeling in my bones that they were going to get along together great! Cal's mum turned to me and said,

"Amber? Would you like to show your sister to the room she's staying in? She'll probably feel better if it's you."

I nodded my head in agreement as Cal sat down on the sofa to chat to his parents and sibling and I took the lead, showing Ellen to her room upstairs. Cal had his own room in the house which is where I would stay when we were there and as I'd been there before, I automatically knew that Ellen would be in the guest bedroom. I showed her into the room, glancing backwards when I heard her gasp. I grinned to myself as I realised that she was in awe of the size and the beauty of the room that she was staying in.

"Wow," she whispered in astonishment, "this is a guestroom?"

"Yeah. It's amazing isn't it?" I answered, looking around the immediate area in admiration. Harry and Rachel were fantastic decorators, making a plain room into an enthralling masterpiece of loveliness. Each time I visited their house, I could never understand how they were able to accomplish such a feat, but their talents were creative physically whilst my talents were always in my writing.

Ellen chuckled at my words.

"Amazing is probably an understatement. Are these people rich or something?" she asked me, a nervous glint in her eyes. I could see that she was starting to feel inferior to them, but she had no need to feel that way.

"Hey, don't worry about it," I told her firmly, "they may appear to be rich, but they're not. They just were exceptionally good at saving throughout their lives, unlike me. They're nice people though, very down to earth. You'll get along with them I'm sure."

I brought my hands up to rub at my temples at that point, wincing as I did so. I'd gotten a terrible headache on the drive over and I'd done my best to ignore it up until that moment but it was starting to throb. Ellen touched me gently on my arm.

"What's wrong?" she asked me softly, concern written clearly on her face.

"I'm ok," I told her, shrugging it off, "it's just a headache. I'll grab some painkillers and it'll disappear soon enough."

Ellen made a noise to indicate that she was appeased by my answer then went to have a look about the room, placing her bag by the foot of the bed before wandering over to the window to take a look outside at the view. Whilst she did that, I pulled a small foil packet from out of my back pocket of my jeans and popped two of the paracetamol tablets into my mouth quickly. I didn't need water to swallow them down luckily. As I shoved the packet back into my pocket, I watched my sister taking everything in, my mind wandering back to my headache. I wasn't sure why, but I'd started to get them more regularly lately. They'd been occurring for several weeks and I hadn't been able to figure out what was causing them. I'd thought maybe it was stress related but I really had nothing to be stressed about at that time in my life. I was happy with everything. I actually had some good news that I wanted to share with Ellen before I told anybody else.

"Before we go back down to the others, I've got something that I need to tell you."

Ellen turned back to me, her gaze curious as she walked over to stand by my side.

"What is it? Is something wrong?"

"No, nothing's wrong. But I *do* have news that I want to share with you before I tell everyone else. You're my sister, my family and we're all we have. Plus, I really wanted to tell someone," I peered into her worried eyes as I took a breath, "I'm pregnant."

The shock that appeared on her face made me chuckle as her jaw slackened.

"You're pregnant? Are you sure?" Ellen asked, obviously not sure she was hearing me right. I nodded my head at her in acknowledgement.

"Yes, I'm very sure. I did three of those pee on a stick tests to make extra sure that I wasn't getting it wrong," I told her matter of factly.

A few seconds passed as my sister processed the news that I had just thrown at her, then she launched herself at me and threw her arms around my neck, squeezing me so tightly that I could barely breathe. I laughed at her excitement, even as I tugged her away from my neck so that I could take in air again. As I looked at her, her whole face was lit up ecstatically at my news.

"Oh my God! You're pregnant!" she cried, a huge smile threatening to split her face in two.

"Ssh!" I chuckled, putting my finger to my lips to encourage her to be quieter, "not so loud! I haven't told Cal yet. You're the first person I've told."

Ellen's smile faltered as she realised what I was telling her, the worried expression she'd had before returning.

"Why haven't you told Cal? Are things ok with you two?"

"Yes! Everything is great with us," I placated, "I haven't told him yet purely because I want to tell him tomorrow. It's a day to celebrate the gift of life tomorrow so what better day to tell him that he's going to be a daddy? I've got him some little presents too of course, but this will be his big present so I'm hoping he takes it well and is happy about the fact we'll be bringing a new life into the world."

"Oh, I think he'll be over the moon with this news! He absolutely adores you Amber, it's obvious to everybody. I'm sure you know it too."

I smiled happily to myself at her words. Yes, I did know. A baby would be perfect to bring into our lives, our future together was going to become complete and I couldn't wait.

*   *   *

Christmas Day.

I awoke to find Cal leaning on his elbow, gazing down at me. He leaned down a little further to kiss me tenderly on my mouth, never tearing his eyes away from my face.

"What?" I giggled, wondering why he was staring at me so much. He kissed me again, grinning cheekily down at me.

"I just like looking at you. Something wrong with that?" he asked, daring me to contradict him. I giggled at his cheesiness even though it made me feel all warm and fuzzy inside. I shook my head as he stroked a finger along my jawline.

"Merry Christmas," I muttered, pulling him down until our lips met once more, heat igniting between us with lust. I moaned into his mouth as he deepened the kiss, his hands exploring my body as they constantly did. I roved my hands along his back, pulling him tighter against me as my hands went lower, wanting him as close to me as possible, skin on skin. He broke the kiss after a while, his gaze locked onto mine.

"I love you Amber. With all that I have."

He said those words to me with such an earnestness that I felt my insides turn to mush at how happy it made me feel.

"I love you too, Cal," I muttered against his lips as I kissed him again. I couldn't wait to tell him about the pregnancy later on that morning. I'd planned to tell him in front of his family because I knew how much Rachel wanted grandchildren. She'd already told me several times since I'd met her that she wanted little children running around her feet once more. I'd decided that if I told him in front of his family, then it would be a bit like a present to them all. Cal and I continued to kiss each other passionately (although we weren't going to take things any further being as it wasn't our house) until someone rapped on our door loudly.

"Wake up lovebirds!" came Ryan's voice from the other side of the door. I chuckled, glancing up at Cal as he rolled his eyes in frustration at his brother's unwanted interruption. We clambered out of the bed to get dressed before we headed down the stairs to join the rest of the family. Everyone was seated in the living room near the Christmas tree and there were two places left on the sofa for Cal and me.

"Right, now that we're all here, let's do presents!" Harry announced, pulling the presents out from under the tree and passing them on to the person whose name was written upon the labels. I opened my presents that were handed to me that were from Cal first whilst everyone else was opening their presents around me. I knew Cal had planned to get me something but I'd received a large gift bag full of presents from him. He'd bought me some fancy notebooks, a couple of books to read and an exquisite heart shaped necklace made from gold with beautiful red gems inset in its core. I placed it around my neck immediately, proud to wear something so lovely.

"Cal, thank you so much. This necklace is beautiful and the books and notebooks are fantastic," I told him, giving him a gentle kiss on the cheek. He smiled back at me, although it faltered a bit as he began to seem nervous. I frowned at him.

"What's wrong?" I asked, wondering what could be bothering him. Hadn't he liked the presents that I'd given to him?

"I need to ask you something," he stated loudly, standing up as he spoke. Everyone in the room fell silent as they watched him pull something from out of his pocket. He went down on one knee and my heart sped up. Was he about to do what I thought he was going to do? I heard Ellen gasp from across the room as she realised what was happening too.

"Amber. As you know well, I have fallen for you completely and utterly. I can no longer imagine my life without you in it, which brings me to this," he held up a small white jewellery box and opened it to reveal a gorgeous gold ring with small diamonds dotted all across the top of the band, "will you stay by my side and make me the happiest man alive by agreeing to become my wife?"

I stared at him, my mouth open as I was rendered speechless momentarily. I took in the ring, his nervous yet hopeful expression and the fact that his whole family were watching me with bated breath as they waited for my answer.

"Yes! Of course it's yes!" I exclaimed, smiling broadly at him. Cal grinned then, the relief washing over him visibly as he slipped the ring onto my finger and swept me up in his arms, kissing me fully on the mouth in full view of his family and my sister. I could hear cheers from the three people sitting around us, their congratulations breaking through my daze. I couldn't believe it. I was engaged!

"Welcome to the family!" Ryan announced, pulling me into a bear hug and lifting me off the ground before allowing his parents to get near me. I laughed at him, his playful nature suiting the moment perfectly.

"Oh, I'm so pleased!" Rachel exclaimed, "You make my boy so happy and I can't think of anyone better for him!"

She gave me a kiss on the cheek and was closely followed by Harry who also gave me a kiss on the cheek. After a few more congratulations from everyone, we all sat back down to continue our Christmas Day. I lifted my hand to admire the new ring that now adorned my ring finger, smiling happily at Cal and snuggling up to him. He was the most kind, wonderful and loving man and I was blessed to have him. I glanced over at Ellen from my place at Cal's side, winking at her so that she could figure out what I was about to do. It seemed to be the perfect moment to tell him about the baby.

"I've actually got another present for you Cal."

The others had been chatting amongst themselves but obviously heard what I'd said because they stopped and glanced over to see what else I'd gotten for him. They were probably wondering what I could possibly give him after receiving my engagement ring from him. I held out a long rectangular shaped present to him, gift wrapped so that he couldn't see what it was until he opened it. My nerves reared their ugly head as I prepared to tell him my news. Although I was reasonably certain that Cal would be happy about the pregnancy, there was still a small voice of doubt in my head telling me to worry that he wouldn't be pleased.

"What is it?" Cal asked me, shaking it a bit to try and figure it out for himself. I chuckled at him.

"Open it and find out," I told him.

He tore the wrapping paper off to reveal a plain cardboard box. I'd managed to find an empty plain box to place the test into so that he didn't get any clues about his 'present' until he took it out. He seemed puzzled, glancing up at me quizzically.

"You need to open the box and look inside," I spoke quietly, waiting anxiously to see what his reaction would be. He pulled the pregnancy test from the box and looked at it, turning it around when he saw the display screen to read what was written there. 'Pregnant' was displayed there clearly for him to see. Cal studied it for a minute before looking away from it and up at me in surprise.

"Are you...? Is this...a pregnancy test? Are you pregnant?" he sputtered, his eyes moving back and forth between me and the test that he held in his hands. I nodded my head slowly at him, still unsure if he was happy or horrified by the news.

"I can't believe it," he whispered. A smile slowly crept its way across his face until he was beaming at me. He grabbed my face between his hands, kissing me passionately.

"I love you so much!"

He kissed me again and pulled me into his arms, his embrace

tender and warm.

"So...you're happy then?" I asked, checking that I was reading his reaction correctly. He extracted himself from his hold on me to gaze into my eyes.

"Of course I am! I'm ecstatic! We're going to have a baby!" he cried, taking a hold of my hands in his. I smiled at him in relief before turning around to see the others staring at us. Rachel had a massive smile on her face so I knew she'd heard the news without me telling her.

"Clearly, you all heard the news so....surprise!" I laughed.

"Oh this is fantastic news!" Rachel exclaimed, rushing over to pull both Cal and myself into a hug. Ryan came over and clapped his brother on the back in congratulations as Ellen came and gave me a high five. That had always been our thing whenever one of us had good news. Harry congratulated us both from his seat, and I got the impression he didn't want to get in the way with everyone else around us so I stood up and strode over to him, wrapping my arms around him.

"Are you pleased?" I asked him softly, wondering what he thought about it all.

"Yes. I am. This has turned out to be one of our best Christmases! I'm gaining a daughter in law and a grandchild all in one day, what's not to love about that?" he told me, a warm smile playing upon his lips. I was pleased to hear that from him. This Christmas truly was turning out to be the best yet and our future looked bright.

CHAPTER THIRTEEN.

Christmas Day with Cal's family turned out to be really nice.

They were very traditional in the sense that we had a proper Turkey roast dinner with all of the trimmings and we had to watch the Queen's Speech when it came on the television. It reminded me of when all of my family were still around and we would spend our Christmas together.

Dinner was a feast! We had roasted turkey, roasted potatoes, Yorkshire puddings, pigs in blankets with a vast array of vegetables and lashings of gravy poured over the top. It was stunning and very delicious. We all had our Christmas crackers to pull, which we did and giggled at each other when we said the silly jokes that came inside of them. The little paper hats that you get in them was a must wear according to Rachel so we had to don those. Ellen and I rolled our eyes at each other as we'd always hated wearing those hats but we did it anyway. After we'd had dinner, Rachel went out to the kitchen and brought back a huge Christmas pudding and placed it onto the table before going back to the kitchen and returning with a trifle bowl and a jug of custard. Once she'd placed them down and sat back down into her seat, she gazed around at us all contentedly.

"I made a Christmas pudding for everyone but as I didn't know if you girls liked it, I also made a boozy strawberry trifle so that there was an alternative," she told us warmly.

"Aww, you didn't have to do that Rachel," Ellen said, the gratitude showing on her face plainly. I was secretly pleased about the trifle too as I wasn't a fan of Christmas pudding. Never had been.

"Of course I did! It doesn't matter if nobody eats it right now because I'm sure it will get demolished at some point during this coming week. Now! Let's enjoy a nice dessert," she announced as she set about dishing up a bowl of whatever everybody fancied for them. She was such a kind lady and I thought it was lovely how she'd thought about Ellen and I and what we might prefer. Not many people I knew would have done that for us.

After we had all finished eating, board games came out and so, we spent the rest of our day playing various games with each other, enjoying the company that we had around us.

Boxing Day followed in very much the same manner. We had yet another large roasted dinner with dessert (and alcoholic drinks) and then that night, we visited the local pub. It was a great night and I thoroughly enjoyed myself, but I also had another one of those annoying headaches that simply would not go away. I'd had paracetamol already but it refused to go, so I headed back to the house early whilst the others stayed to have a few more drinks. Cal had wanted to return to the house with me, but I refused to let him miss out on spending time with his family by taking care of me. There wasn't much that he could do anyway as it was a headache so I pointed that out to him and told him I would see him later when he got back.

Even when I'd reached the house, Cal kept messaging me to see how I was so I eventually had to tell him that I was going to go to bed so that he would give me some peace. It was nice to know that he cared but he didn't need to fuss over me. I wanted him to have fun, whether or not I was there. I must have fallen asleep in the end because I woke up a few hours later to find Cal in the bed beside me. I felt nauseous and my head was pounding against the walls of my skull. I headed down the hallway to the bathroom, praying that I was going to be sick.

Unfortunately, my wish wasn't granted. I ended up being very sick, leaning over the toilet as I vomited, crying a little to myself as I felt awful. It didn't take long before I felt someone's arms around my shoulders and my hair being pulled back from my face.

"There there," Rachel's voice soothed, "let it out."

She stayed there with me whilst I threw up, holding onto me and keeping my face hair free until I was finished. I slumped down onto the floor as my knees gave out beneath me and she went to fetch me a damp flannel. She wiped at my face gently, not saying anything for a few minutes. The way she did it was so caring, I felt like crying again. I missed my own mother terribly so it was nice to have this small comfort, even though it was from Cal's mum and not my own. She peered down at me once my face was clean and spoke softly to me.

"Is it out of your system now do you think?"

"I think so," I replied weakly, "but I'm not sure what caused it. I know with being pregnant you can get morning sickness so I guess it could be that but I've also still got this awful headache that won't go away so do you think it could be that that brought my sickness on?"

"It's possible. A truly bad headache or migraine can make a person unwell but if it's that bad, I suggest you get seen by a doctor considering your condition. It might be that you need an extra nutrient or vitamin of some kind that you're lacking without realising. They'll be able to put you right. Come on, let's get you back to bed and see if you can rest up for a couple more hours," Rachel said, helping me to my feet.

I glanced guiltily in her direction.

"I'm sorry that I woke you up, Rachel."

She waved a hand at me dismissing my comment.

"Don't worry about that! It's never a nice thing when you're poorly and it's nice to know there's someone with you. I've been through it over the years with my boys so it doesn't bother me. I would just rather know that you're alright. Now, off you pop and get some sleep. I'll see you in the morning," she told me, before turning and heading off into the direction of her own bedroom. I stood and watched her go, then sighing to myself, I headed back to Cal's room and attempted to go back to sleep, eventually falling into a fitful restless dream.

I woke up the next morning and groaned to myself into the pillow. The headache was *still* there, thumping away at my head like a bass drum had been set up in there. I felt utterly rubbish. The nausea had passed a little but my stomach still felt as though I'd gone five rounds with a boxer whilst taking all of their hits to the tummy. Cal had already disappeared and when I looked at the time, I realised why. It was just after ten o'clock in the morning! I'd slept most of the morning away. I pushed myself up into a sitting position gingerly, rubbing at my temples with my fingers and willing the headache to go away. Was this what happened during a pregnancy? If it was, then I wasn't looking forward to the next nine months of my life.

Cal walked into the room then, peeking his head around the door to see if I was awake, I'm sure. When he saw that I was sat up, he came into the room and perched himself on the edge of the bed and looked at me with concern.

"Mum told me about last night. How are you feeling now?" he asked me.

"Honestly? Not great. I don't feel sick anymore but this stupid headache hasn't gone anywhere," I replied honestly.

"Mum told me I need to get you checked out by a doctor just to make sure that everything is ok with you. You know, for peace of mind. I've already rang your doctors for you and we've got an appointment booked for you for tomorrow morning so we'll head back home today."

I stared at him in dismay, guilt taking over my emotions. Great, now I was ruining the time we had with his parents.

"You can't do that Cal! We're supposed to be here all week!" I cried, wondering what I should do but Cal shook his head.

"I know but your health is more important. We will have plenty more Christmases in the future so don't worry yourself over it. When you're up and ready to go, we'll head back so that you can get some more sleep before tomorrow ok?" he said, not leaving me much room to argue with him. I just nodded my head and waited for him to leave the room before I got up and sorted myself out.

When I walked down the stairs, I met Cal at the bottom.

"Is your bag ready to go in the car?" he asked, waiting for me to get past him before stepping up onto the bottom step of the staircase.

"Yes, it's on the bed. Are you sure about this? I might feel better soon and this will all have been silly."

"Of course I'm sure. If everything is alright and we're just panicking for no reason, then we can always come back for a couple of days over New Year can't we?" he asked, reminding me how simple things could be. I sighed again miserably as he bounded up the stairs to collect our bags. I know his heart was in the right place but I still felt guilty for tearing him away from his family.

I strode into the living room quietly, glancing around me at the others dejectedly.

"I'm so sorry that we're leaving and going home. Truly I am," I apologised to the room as a whole. Rachel stood and came over to me, wrapping me into a tight hug.

"Don't you worry about us, Amber. Just get yourself checked and better ok?"

I turned to Ellen, sorrow in my heart. I was ruining her Christmas week too by going home.

"Ellen, I'm so sorry that I'm ruining your week," I muttered, my eyes downcast because I didn't want to look into her eyes. Ellen smiled at me, coming over to take me into her arms as well.

"You're not, don't worry. I'm going to stay here and then if you come back, we'll be able to spend New Year together!"

I gazed at her curiously as I replied,

"You're staying?"

"Yep," she nodded, "if you don't come back, Ryan has offered to drive me back home. Harry and Rachel have been really kind and told me that I can stay here for the time we'd arranged and as Doug is away, I agreed. I hope that's ok with you though?"

"Yes, of course it is!" I cried, relief flooding through me, "I was so worried that I was going to be ruining Christmas for you too but I'm glad you're staying. You'll have fun."

Cal came into the living room after several minutes to tell me that our bags were in the car and that it was time to head off. We said our goodbyes to everyone, hugging and kissing each other as we did so. Then, we clambered into the car and drove home.

It had only taken us just over an hour to complete our journey back home but by the time we arrived, I felt exhausted. Cal hadn't spoken to me much on the drive back, instead just watching me out of the corner of his eye as he drove, a concerned frown upon his lips. I helped him take our bags inside the house then told him that I wasn't going to go for a lie down for a bit. Cal acknowledged me and I headed upstairs.

I knew he was probably starting to worry about me a bit but my head was throbbing and I was starting to feel nauseated again and I just wanted to go to sleep. I threw my clothes off and onto the floor once I reached my bedroom, not caring that I left them on the floor and then pulled on my nightshirt before falling onto the bed and falling asleep almost instantaneously.

When I came to a few hours later, I found Cal lying in the bed beside me with a lamp on on his side, reading a book.

"What time is it?" I asked groggily, moving closer to him so that I could curl up against his side without disturbing his reading but as soon as he heard me, he put the book down and turned to face me, placing his arm around my shoulders to snuggle me in closer to him. Aah, that was bliss to me.

"It's nearly seven," he answered, "how are you feeling now?"

I gasped at him in shock.

"*Seven?!* You mean, I've slept all afternoon?" I couldn't believe it. I'd never slept that much in my life! What had gotten into me? I shook my head at myself until I realised to my joy, that the headache had finally disappeared!

"The headache has gone at last so I guess all that sleep has helped," I admitted sheepishly. I felt bad that I'd slept that much but as it had gotten rid of my headache that had been plaguing me, then I didn't feel *too* badly about it. "What have you done with your afternoon whilst I was trying to be Sleeping Beauty?"

Cal picked up the book he'd been reading when I awoke and showed it to me.

"Reading," he said matter of factly as he showed me the liberal chunk of text he'd read whilst I'd been sleeping. My eyes grew wide.

"Have you been there next to me all this time?"

Cal nodded his head at me, squeezing my shoulder tightly with his hand.

"Yeah. I wanted to be nearby in case you needed me. I've been pretty worried about you," he confessed. I gazed up at his face, taking in the expression of concern he couldn't hide.

"Yeah, I noticed you keeping an eye on me in the car," I told him softly, "I'm sorry that I worried you. I didn't mean to."

"I know you didn't," he replied, "but that doesn't mean I'm not going to worry about you. I love you and I want you to be alright."

I took a hold of his hand in mine as I lay against him, my head resting on his shoulder.

"I know babe. I'm sure everything will be fine. It's most likely pregnancy related or I've caught a stomach bug from somewhere and that's it. I'll get checked out by the doctor tomorrow and everything will be alright. I'm sure of it," I told him boldly, settling into his arms comfortably.

Boy, was I wrong.

CHAPTER FOURTEEN.

The next morning, we arrived at the doctor's office early and checked in at the reception.

There weren't many people there which was probably because it was Christmas week, so we chose to sit in the far corner of the waiting room as the magazine rack stood nearby and we could read something whilst we waited. We had just sat down when a voice came over the tannoy, calling for me.

"Amber Ackles, room 3 please. That's Amber Ackles, room 3."

"Do you want me to come with you or stay here?" Cal asked as I rose from my chair.

"You can come in babe, it's fine," I told him, taking a hold of his hand as we walked down a short corridor until we found a door with a large number three on it and went into our designated room. I walked through the door first, closely followed by Cal who closed the door behind us. The doctor was sat at a desk unit in front of a computer and there were two extra chairs by the side of the desk that were unoccupied. The doctor looked up at us and gave me a tight smile as I took a seat nearest the desk and Cal took the seat next to me.

"How can we help you today Miss Ackles?" she asked, a disinterested look upon her face. I supposed I couldn't blame her, it was Christmas week after all. She probably didn't want to be there but she was, so she could at least pretend to be interested even when she wasn't. I cleared my throat, glancing towards Cal for support.

"It probably sounds silly to you but I keep getting headaches and they can be quite painful. They last for hours and recently, I had one that was so bad that I was physically sick. I've also recently discovered that I'm pregnant so I thought maybe it was just to do with that?" I told her, hoping it wasn't serious and she would let me go home thinking I was a fool to worry.

"OK," the doctor said, her eyes lighting up with curiosity, "can I ask how long you've been experiencing these headaches for? And also, when did you discover that you were with child?"

I thought about my answers carefully, trying to get the information as accurate as possible.

"Well, the headaches have been happening for perhaps four or five weeks? I think. And I found out about the pregnancy a couple of weeks before Christmas. I've already had it confirmed that I'm pregnant but I didn't tell my partner Cal here about the pregnancy until Christmas Day because I wanted it to be a surprise present. I took the test three times to be sure," I stated confidently. Cal's fingers brushed against mine as the doctor frowned.

"So, from what you're telling me, the headaches seem to have started before you fell pregnant?" she asked enquiringly.

I thought hard about it, I wasn't too sure. I hadn't paid all that much attention to the headaches when they'd started because when they'd occurred, they didn't last long. It had only been when they started to become more frequent that I truly took notice of them.

"I'm not sure but yes, I believe so. It actually may have been longer than a few weeks. Possibly even two months now that I'm really thinking about it," I told her. I heard Cal's intake of breath beside me but chose to ignore him. I had a feeling he wouldn't be happy that I hadn't told him I'd been suffering with these headaches for such a long time but I honestly hadn't taken too much notice of them. They'd come, they'd gone. End of. And then they'd gotten more frequent, the pain of them increasing each and every time.

"OK," the doctor said, "it's possible that there is nothing to worry about here as headaches can be quite common during the first trimester of a pregnancy but I'm just going to take a look at you to be on the safe side alright?"

"Oh OK, yeah," I replied, watching her as she picked up a small torch from near the back of her desk. She stood and walked over to the wall where she flicked a switch, plunging the room into semi-darkness due to the grey skies that could be seen through the sky light in the ceiling. When she'd come back to us, she pulled her chair over until it was directly in front of me, sitting down upon it and raising the torch up so that she could shine the light in my eyes.

"Right, I'm just going to have a look at your eyes using this light, Miss Ackles. I apologise for the brightness but it is a necessary evil," the doctor said kindly, her frosty exterior finally thawing a little bit. She turned the torch on and shone it directly into my right eye. Yep, it was blinding. She checked my eye for what felt like an hour although it was most likely only a few minutes and then she shone the light into my left eye, repeating her examination whilst I tried to regain my sight in the right eye.

From what I could see, the doctor was frowning. That couldn't be good news, I thought to myself as the doctor got up and went to turn the lighting back on again. As she came and sat back down in front of her desk, I could see she looked pensive and I wondered what was going through her mind at that moment. The doctor then turned to Cal and addressed him as thought I weren't sat right in front of her.

"Has Miss Ackles experienced any issues recently regarding her memory? Or her motor skill functions? Has she been clumsy at all?"

"Erm, why are you asking Cal and not me?" I asked confused. This was weird and I knew it.

"I'm asking your partner Miss Ackles because if there have been any noticeable changes such as the things I've just mentioned, then he will be the most likely to have seen them. You may not have noticed anything you were doing is different to before so I need to ask someone close to you," the doctor explained to me.

I turned anxiously to face Cal, taking in his screwed up face as he tried to think if anything had changed with me over the past little while.

"Cal? Have you noticed anything?" I prompted when he started to take a bit too long to answer. He cleared his throat, casting a guilty look in my direction as he spoke, as though he didn't want to upset me.

"Well, she has been a bit forgetful lately which she isn't usually. Like sometimes it's something small, another time it's something big. Either way, it's not like Amber to forget *any*thing normally so yeah I've noticed that. And she's always been clumsy, although now that I think about it, she *has* been slightly more clumsy than she usually is too. Why? What do you think is going on doc?" Cal asked, squeezing my hand gently because he could tell I was starting to get scared. The fact that my hand was starting to shake was probably a dead giveaway. I was glad that I'd asked him to come in there with me after all. Why was this doctor asking these questions? What did she think was happening? The doctor turned back to her computer and typed something using the keyboard before turning back to me. I swallowed hard at the expression on her face. Something was wrong. Very wrong.

"Miss Ackles, after looking into your eyes, there appears to be some pressure building behind them. Because of that, I would like to send you to see a neurologist and also to have a scan so that we can see what is happening inside your head. Your appointment will come through in a week or two but if you have not received your appointment by the end of the second week, I would like you to call and let me know so that I can get that sorted swiftly for you. From there, we will be able to check you over and see what's happening," the doctor told me calmly, her composure belying the concern that shone through her eyes.

I had to see a neurologist? Why? This was starting to sound

serious and I was getting very worried. Since when did appointments come through that quickly? And why did I have to let her know if it hadn't arrived by the second week? What exactly was the rush here?

"What do you think it is? Why do I need to see a neurologist?" I asked her, gripping Cal's hand tightly, almost afraid to let go of it. I glanced at him out of the corner of my eye, noticing that the colour had drained from his face, worry lines beginning to pinch at his mouth. The doctor gazed steadily at me, hesitating. Why was she hesitating? What was she holding back?

"Well, as I have already said, there appears to be pressure building up behind your eyes," she began slowly, "I need you to be examined by a neurologist to determine whether it is something significant that we need to be concerned about or whether it is something benign that we can fix to alleviate the pressure quickly for you. Either way, we need to get you checked by a specialist."

"OK, I understand that but you still haven't told me what you think it might be. If it's something significant, what sort of thing do you mean? What would be classed as significant?" I asked. I knew I was probably being annoying but damn it, I wanted her to answer me and be honest.

"The sort of things we would be looking for would be a glioma," the doctor replied. I rolled my eyes impatiently at her then. What was a glioma for crying out loud?

"What is one of those in normal person speak?"

"It means that we could be looking for the possibility of a brain tumour," the doctor answered quietly, watching us as that news sank in. What? A brain tumour? No way. Surely that wasn't possible…was it? I thought of something else at that moment.

"Will the examination or scan affect the baby at all?" I asked, still trying to comprehend what she'd told me. The doctor shook her head at my question.

"No, your baby shouldn't be affected by the testing so please don't worry about that at the moment. Now, whilst you're here, would you like to talk about your current condition or would you prefer to come back at another time to discuss that? I can understand that you must be feeling a bit overwhelmed at this point."

I opened and closed my mouth like a goldfish, unable to find the words to answer her. Luckily, Cal stepped in and spoke for me.

"Maybe we should arrange it for another time please?"

"Of course. Just make an appointment with the receptionist on your way out. Do you know how far along you are?" she asked, obviously trying to give me something good to walk away with from there. I shook my head.

"That's OK, we can figure that out for you now if you would like? Do you know when your last menstruation was?"

I thought about it briefly, answering her in a monotone voice. A dead calm had started to seep through me, as though I were seeing things from someone else's view. She sat and worked it out for a few minutes before smiling brightly at both Cal and myself.

"Congratulations! It would appear that you are at about the six week mark! That would put your due date at around the 15th or 16th of August! When you come back, we shall discuss things in more detail and we will arrange for your twelve week scan to be booked in as well ok?" the doctor told us, that false smile on her face already grating on my nerves.

"Thanks doc. I'm going to take her home now. Thanks for your time," Cal muttered, holding out his hand to offer the doctor a hand shake. She took his hand and they shook, before Cal reached down and helped me up, steering me out of the office and into the reception so that we could book our appointment about the baby. I allowed Cal to go ahead and book the appointment whilst I hung back, fear rising inside me like a tidal wave. I knew the doctor had said there may not be anything to worry about but that didn't appease me when I knew that she was sending me to see a neurologist because she'd seen something in me that had concerned her enough to do that.

Cal trudged over to me after booking the appointment and pressed his hand against my lower back, gently initiating a stroll outside back towards the car. I was grateful that he hadn't said anything to me yet about what we'd been told otherwise I would have probably cried all over him in public. As we rode home in the car, I glanced at Cal a couple times, unsure as to what he was thinking. I could see a tic moving in his jaw and he seemed to be angry. I didn't know why he was angry but maybe that was how he was dealing with the news we'd received. As soon as the car pulled into the driveway and came to a stop, I jumped out quickly and headed into the house.

I didn't wait for Cal because I wanted to go and do something. Anything. Just to keep myself busy. I strode into the kitchen in a daze, turning the kettle on and fetching the hot chocolate from out of the cupboard. I scooped spoonfuls of the powdered chocolate into my favourite mug and waited for the kettle to boil. It was a cold day and I needed to warm up, inside and out. I called to Cal when I heard him come through the door to see if he wanted a drink. He came into the kitchen to join me, standing in the doorway and leaning against the doorjamb.

"I'll have a coffee please."

I set about making the coffee for him. After the kettle had boiled, I poured our drinks and stirred them, saying nothing as I did so. Cal stole up behind me, wrapping his arms around my waist and kissed me on my neck gently.

"I know you're worried about what the doctor said but remember what else she said, that it may not be anything."

"I know," I muttered back, leaning into him and allowing him to hold me tighter, "I'm more worried about you right now though. You seemed to be quite angry in the car."

He stepped to the side, picking up his coffee and taking a sip before answering me.

"I'm sorry for being angry babe. I'm not angry exactly, I think that I was a bit nervous about what the doctor said. I know I shouldn't jump to conclusions and I'm not, so don't think I am. I'm more frustrated that we have to wait for you to be seen by this neurologist. The doctor blatantly saw something which she thought needed to be checked so why wait? Why not just get you straight to the hospital, have the scan and find out what's going on?"

"I know," I soothed, rubbing his arm lightly as I stayed in his embrace, "I'd like to know too but there's no point working ourselves up over it until we know exactly what we're dealing with. Tests take time to be made so I think we're quite lucky that we're getting one so soon."

Cal eyed me cautiously, watching as I sipped at my hot chocolate.

"How are you able to be so calm?" he asked, confused.

"I'm not sure," I admitted, "I don't feel calm but I also know that worrying about it all isn't going to do me any favours. Yes, the doctor said that there's the possibility of a brain tumour but there's also the possibility that it's something minor that can be fixed easily. I've got too much to look forward to in my life right now so I'm not going to panic until I know what's happening. So how about we forget about it for now and enjoy the rest of the day together? I am officially your fiancée now and I'm also carrying your child. We've got a lot going for us so let's enjoy ourselves right here, right now. What do you say?"

He smiled warmly down at me.

"I love you Amber Ackles."

"I love you to Callum Jacobson."

CHAPTER FIFTEEN.

The following two weeks passed by quickly.

I'd received my letter from the hospital inviting me to go and see a neurologist during the second week of January. I realised that by the time I went to see the neurologist, I would be two months pregnant! Whilst we waited for the appointment, we celebrated our New Year quietly together at home, watching movies and making love. Ellen had called me a couple of times and I'd told her that I was going to have a few tests but I didn't tell her what the possibilities were. I didn't see the point in making her worry over me, especially if it ended up being that nothing was a major issue. I was still getting the headaches and I was still feeling nauseous although I started putting the nausea down to the pregnancy. I'd been doing some research on my laptop and apparently it is common for women in their first trimester to feel sick and most likely, they were physically sick. Admittedly, I was feeling grotty most days but I did my best to ignore it. Tiredness had started to play a part in my life now as I was constantly tired. Was that normal? I didn't know but I slept all the time. I decided that I might as well rest as much as I could before I got bigger with this baby.

I'd found myself stroking my belly on occasion, wondering whether I would be having a little boy or a little girl. Cal had taken to kissing me goodnight each night and then kissing my stomach, saying goodnight to our little bun in the oven. We'd even started referring to the baby as Little Bun. It had seemed like a good idea when we were discussing the child one night and what we thought they may be like.

"Do you want a boy or a girl?" I asked Cal, a couple of days before my appointment would be upon us.

"I don't mind babe, as long as they're healthy. Do you have a preference?"

"I kind of want a little girl," I admitted, giggling a little at his expression, "Don't get me wrong, I don't mind what we have but if I had to choose, I'd have a girl."

"Why?" Cal chuckled, placing his hand on my thigh and splaying his fingers wide. It felt nice.

"Well…I love the fact that they can wear cute little dresses and you can do their hair nicely and I don't know really, I just fancy a girl."

Cal leaned down, placing his head close to my tummy as he spoke to our baby that was growing inside of me each day.

"Can you be a girl please Little Bun?" Cal said to my stomach, "your mummy wants a girl. Daddy doesn't mind but we don't want to upset mummy now do we?"

I laughed at him, catching a hold of his shirt and pulled him up to my level.

"If you don't want to upset mummy then can mummy have a kiss from daddy please?"

"Yes ma'am," Cal growled against my lips as he captured my mouth into a passionate kiss.

*   *   *

The day of the appointment came and we set off for the hospital.

I tried to keep a calm composure as we strode through the hospital doors but inside, my nerves were starting to get to me. I wanted to stay strong for Cal but I was faltering. I shook my head at myself, trying to clear away the cobwebs that threatened to take control of my mind. Stop worrying, I scolded myself. Once inside, we consulted the letter that had arrived in the post to see which department we needed to go to, and then that was where we headed.

After finding where we needed to be, I checked myself in at the reception desk and sat down to wait. And wait. And wait. Finally, what seemed like hours later, my name was called out so Cal and I made our way to the room that the receptionist had pointed to on arrival. We had a male doctor this time around with a mass of greying hair upon his head ready to greet me. He introduced himself to us as Dr Bradley with a warm smile and a handshake.

"Welcome," Dr Bradley greeted, "have you had it explained to you what we are doing here today and what we are looking for?"

"Not completely," Cal answered him, "we were told that Amber has got pressure behind her eyes and the doctor told us that the sort of things you look for are brain tumours. Other than that, we're a bit in the dark."

Dr Bradley sighed, seemingly annoyed at our previous doctor.

"Your doctor has sent you here with an urgent referral for testing so today I shall be conducting a neurological exam to discover more about what is going on in your head. Have you ever heard of gliomas?" he asked gently.

"Yes, the doctor who referred us said that it's a brain tumour," I replied quietly. My fear was growing the longer I stayed in there.

"They're right but there are many different types of brain tumours. Some are benign little tumours that can be removed easily with a short recovery time. However, some tumours can be quite large and depending on what type of tumour it is, some can be very serious indeed. However, it could be none of the above and it could be something extremely simple such as a sinus infection or something similar so until we do all of our testing, there is no way to know for sure so I'd like to run a few tests on you to rule out a few things and then arrange a scan for us to get a clear image of your brain and know exactly how you are. Does that sound good?" Dr Bradley asked me brightly.

I was liking his positive attitude so much. He was straight to the point and explained himself. So far, this doctor was making me feel as though I would be well looked after and that went a long way in making me relax a bit. I nodded my head at him to answer his question and so, Dr Bradley checked on his computer screen on the desk next to him as he took a quick look at my notes.

"Now it says in your notes here that you are pregnant, is that correct?" he asked me.

"Yes that's right," I told him, casting a small smile at Cal whilst checking on him to see that he was doing alright. So far so good.

"In that case, it will probably be safer for us to run an MRI scan for you as that will be better for the baby. There are always some risks during these types of tests when you're pregnant but it will be your best option. I'm going to go ahead and get that all set up for you once we're done in here, but first I'm going to run a few tests to gather some more information so that I can determine if your doctor's suspicions were well founded or not," Dr Bradley told us firmly.

The rest of that appointment passed in a blur. Dr Bradley did a few tests on me, *hmm*ing and *aah*ing every so often. It made me anxious to know why he kept making those noises. Had he found something? If so, what? I kept praying to myself that he wouldn't find anything too bad with me. I really hoped he wouldn't. As we came to the end, Dr Bradley had leaned back in his chair and informed my fiancé and I that he thought my local doctor had been right to refer me to him. He told me that the MRI scan would be scheduled straightaway as it needed doing as soon as possible. He asked us to follow him to the reception, which we did, and he spoke to the receptionist to arrange my MRI scan for as soon as possible. I felt like I was in a daze and when I peeked at Cal, I could tell that he was feeling the same way.

A letter was printed off and handed to me, so I peered down at it to see that my MRI scan had been scheduled for the next day. Just one day away. Dr Bradley turned back to me and shook my hand before reaching out and shaking Cal's hand as well.

"Try not to worry until we know more. I'll see you both tomorrow."

With that, he hurried off, ready to see in his next patient. Cal took a hold of my hand and we walked back out of the hospital, not letting go of me until we reached the car. I watched Cal as he placed his arms around my shoulders, pulling me tightly into him. I embraced him, resting my head on his shoulder as I took in a deep breath. Hot tears pricked at the corners of my eyes, threatening to break the dam that had been holding them back until now.

"This is getting serious isn't it?" I whispered, knowing Cal could hear me.

He stroked my hair, hesitating before he replied.

"It seems to be, yeah," he admitted, "having a scan that soon can't be a good sign babe."

That was it. Those words were what pushed me over the edge and the floodgates opened in my eyes. Cal held me close as I cried into his shoulder, unable to stop myself. I was frightened of what was going to be found the next day. Why was this all happening so fast? Why was this happening at all? I sobbed and sobbed, clinging onto my man and soaking his shirt. He didn't say anything. He simply held me and let me cry, allowing me to know that he was there for me. I eventually calmed down, the tears ceasing to cascade down my face at last. I sniffled miserably as I looked up at Cal.

He cupped my cheek, using his thumb to swipe away some of my tears that lingered upon my cheeks and pressed a kiss to my forehead lovingly.

"Let's go home," he whispered into my hair.

We got into the car and drove. That journey felt like a long one but I felt comforted slightly with the knowledge that Cal was there with me. He placed his hand on my thigh for the entire ride, only moving it when he had to change gears but it went straight back onto my thigh as soon as it could. He didn't speak but that was his way of letting me know he was there. That he loved me. He knew I needed that small comfort and I was grateful that he knew what I needed just then.

When we finally made it home, I went inside and plonked myself down on the sofa. I wasn't sure what I was supposed to say or do now.

"We will get through this Amber," Cal assured me, sitting down next to me, "I'm always going to help you through anything and we can do it together."

"Yeah I know, and thank you," I said, "it's just that…I feel like this must be something serious if they're rushing everything to be done so soon? I mean, when have the doctors ever rushed to get answers? I know there's a lot more treatments out there these days so I should be alright, regardless of what they find. I know that, but it's scary to think that I might have a brain tumour. You know?"

Cal agreed, the very real fear showing in his eyes making me realise that all of our plans for the future may change. I hoped not but I had to face the possibility.

*   *   *

The next day was scan day.

All of the previous day, I had busied myself about the house by tidying and reading books. Cal had remained nearby at all times, not mentioning the appointment or anything else because he knew that I needed the time to process what was happening. We pretended that everything was alright that night, talking more about our Little Bun. It was nice discussing our future, our wedding that we wanted and our child. I wasn't really showing just yet but I knew I would be soon enough. This issue with the head-aches had come into my life at a bad time. I didn't want to be ill whilst I was pregnant. From everything I'd heard, pregnancy could be quite uncomfortable so being ill at the same time, just sounded like a living nightmare.

We left for the hospital again, both of us very quiet as the trepi-dation grew within both of us. When we got there, I was taken to a side room and explained to what was about to happen now that I was there. They asked if I agreed with doing everything that they had told me so I said yes. How else was I supposed to find out what was wrong with me otherwise?

I was taken into a room where the MRI machine was. Cal couldn't go in with me at this point so he waited outside for me, and I already knew that he would be constantly checking his watch to see how long I would be taking. The machine it-self looked massive. It was a large tubular machine with a hole at one end which I presumed was where I would have to go in. I'd been warned that it made loud noises during the testing so I was given a pair of headphones to place over my ears to protect them. It all felt surreal but I knew it needed to be done. I laid down where and when they told me to before I was placed in-side the machine. Here we go, I thought to myself. I took a deep breath to steady myself and allowed the doctors to do what they needed to do.

*   *   *

The MRI scan had been completed and whatever they had found had resulted in them performing a needle biopsy whilst I was in there (with my consent) so that they could test a tissue sample to get more information. I was told that I would be able to go home the same day but that I would need to wait and rest in one of the hospital beds until I was given the all clear to go home. Cal had been waiting for me in the waiting area the whole time that

I was being tested on and so, when we came out, he followed me onto a ward where I was placed into a bed until we'd been seen by the doctor and discharged.

"How are you feeling?" Cal asked, brushing his fingers across mine. I moved my eyes over to see his. I grunted.

"I feel rubbish. Between these tests and this pregnancy, I want to hibernate away from the world and never come out again," I told him honestly. I truly felt awful right then. After a couple of hours with nurses coming in to check on me and take my vitals, Dr Bradley finally came to see me. I was feeling a tad bit annoyed at that point, why had he taken so long?

"Miss Ackles, thankyou for coming in today and having the scan and biopsy taken. I've had a check of your MRI scan and there does appear to be a mass on your brain which is what has been causing your symptoms that you've been experiencing. We have taken a sample of the tissue so that we can discover exactly what type of glioma we are dealing with so that we can give you the correct course of treatment. These results should be back within the next week so once I've received and studied them, I'll call you in so that we can discuss your options," Dr Bradley paused momentarily before continuing on, "I apologise I have not been able to bring you better news today. I would like you to rest and take things easy until we have your results back alright?"

I gulped, trying to take it all in.

"Yeah that's fine but can I just double check that you just said that I do have a brain tumour?" I asked bluntly. I needed to make sure that I hadn't mistaken him during his long speech.

"Yes, I'm afraid that that is what we are looking at Miss Ackles. It would explain the headaches, the forgetfulness and the clumsiness that you've been experiencing. We shall release you shortly and then you'll be able to go home and relax until I call you in. It's been nice to see you again," Dr Bradley told me and with that, he was gone.

Cal sat down on the bed next to me, gazing down at me with bleary eyes. His face was pale and he visibly swallowed although I could tell that he was trying hard not to show his fear. I squeezed his fingers in my hand.

"We'll be alright Cal. We know what we're dealing with now and once the results of my biopsy come back, then we'll be able to start fixing it. Don't forget, we've got a baby on the way so I need to be all healthy by the time he or she arrives," I smiled at him, attempting to make him feel better. I received a wan smile in return.

"Do you know how amazing you are?" he asked me, focusing fully on me now. I blushed at that, I could feel my cheeks starting to burn up.

"That's very nice of you to say babe, but I haven't done anything," I chuckled at him.

"Yes you have. You've just been told some bad news and you're staying positive. To me, that's amazing," Cal declared. I shrugged my shoulders.

"There's nothing I can do about it right now and I got all of my tears out yesterday with you so I might as well be positive about things until we know more. We've still got our wedding to look forward to and Little Bun will be with us before the end of the year. We've got a lot of good things going on and I can't wait for our little family to start."

Cal kissed me then, fully on my mouth as he crashed his lips against mine and devoured me. I could tell that he was pouring all of his love into that kiss and I sighed contentedly against his lips, proud to call this man my own. I loved him so much.

A few more hours passed and I was discharged. By that time, I couldn't wait to get out of there. I'd always hated staying in hospitals so it didn't take long for me to leave to go home. For a treat, we picked up a Chinese takeaway on our way home so that we could have a nice meal without having to cook. It had been a long, draining day for the both of us so takeaway it was. I chose a beef chowmein for myself whilst Cal had kung po chicken and seaweed. When he ordered what he was having, I'd looked at him in surprise.

"What?" he asked me innocently.

"You're having seaweed with kung po chicken?" I asked in disbelief. It was such an odd combination of food to have and he didn't appear as though he understood why I'd asked.

"Yeah it's nice," he smiled, "you can try some of mine. Then you'll see I'm right."

I laughed at him then, knowing he was attempting to lighten the dark mood that had encircled us since we'd left the hospital.

"Why would I ever agree that you're right? Didn't you know that women are always right and men are always wrong?"

"Men aren't always wrong," Cal disclosed to me conspiratorially.

"Yes they are," I laughed again, "didn't you know that even when they're right about something, men are usually wrong? Everybody knows that."

He chortled at my silliness, standing up when our names were called to collect our order from the counter.

"Come on babe, let's go home," he said, taking my hand as we walked back towards the car. Even though that day had been quite horrible, it was still going to end on a good note purely because I was with Cal and he made me feel as though I could face anything that life threw at me. We snuggled up together on the sofa that night, eating our takeaway and watching rubbish television. To someone else, it may have seemed boring but to me, I was happy. Life was about enjoying the little things and not taking them for granted.

CHAPTER SIXTEEN.

The day after my scan and biopsy, I called Sally and asked her if she wanted to come over for dinner that night for a catch up. I hadn't seen her since before we'd gone to Cal's parents for Christmas and I knew that we were way past due a chat. She agreed to come over and said she'd be at ours for six o'clock.

Cal offered to cook dinner for us all so that I could relax and chat to Sally when she arrived without having to think about cooking. I thanked him, knowing I was lucky to have a man who was willing to cook for us and my friend. I was currently in between books and was supposed to have started on my next one by now but what with everything that had been going on, I hadn't begun writing yet. Sally knew there was something wrong with me but I hadn't had the courage to tell her. She already knew that I was pregnant and engaged to Cal because I'd messaged her on Christmas Day to tell her my news but since then, we hadn't spoken all that much. I found myself looking forward to spending some time with my friend. I'd missed her.

During the day, I did a few odd jobs about the house such as putting the washing on and then hanging it up to dry on the airers, tidying up the living room and plumping the cushions and I also did a bit of dusting on the wooden surfaces. They were all just small jobs but they were time consuming and kept me busy. Cal went out shopping so that he could get the ingredients to make a Jamaican chicken jambalaya for dinner whilst I stayed behind and finished up making our house look more presentable for visitors. When I was done, I sat down on the sofa with a new book that I'd recently purchased and began to read. It was a psychological thriller about a serial killer who took the lives of those whose birthdays corresponded with each month. It was based on the zodiac signs and I was gripped from the start. I barely noticed when Cal arrived back home, prepping the ingredients in the kitchen for our meal as I was so engrossed.

A while later, I could hear him chortling to himself. I glanced up to see him stood in the kitchen doorway, drying his hands on a tea towel as he studied me from his position.

"What?" I asked, wondering why he was laughing at me.

"Do you know what time it is?" he asked smiling widely. I picked up my mobile phone from next to me to see that the time displayed on the screen said half five in the afternoon. My eyes widened as I shot a look back at Cal.

"Have I been reading all this time?" I gasped, shocked I'd managed to become so interested in the book I'd been reading that I'd lost track of time. Cal nodded his head, coming over to me and pressing a kiss against my lips.

"Yeah, but you're adorable to watch. The facial expressions you pull when you're reading is fascinating to watch babe. You're so open with your emotions," he told me, "but I do think maybe you should put it down for a while now being as Sally is going to be here soon."

I smiled sheepishly up at him.

"It probably would be a good idea," I agreed, reluctantly putting my book down. It seems silly but whenever I get into a book that I'm truly enjoying, I don't like to take breaks from it until I've devoured it from start to finish. The zodiac killer book was one of those stories. I got up to stretch my legs and went into the kitchen to see how the jambalaya was coming along. (I didn't have a clue how to make it or how you're supposed to cook it but I thought I'd check on it anyway and pretend like I did know).

At six o'clock on the dot, the doorbell rang. I greeted Sally at the door and invited her in, giving her a hug in welcome as she came inside. Cal called hello to her from the kitchen whilst he carried on with cooking our food and I asked fetched Sally a glass of wine whilst I had a lemonade. Sitting down next to each other on the sofa, we began talking.

"Hey, so what's going on with you lately?" Sally asked me, concern evident in her tone of voice. I took a breath before answering her, gazing her directly in the eye.

"Do you remember me complaining about my headaches before Christmas? I kept getting them all the time right?" when she nodded her head in acknowledgment, I continued on, "well I became really poorly during Christmas week so because of the pregnancy, both Cal and his parents recommended that I go and see a doctor to get checked over so that we could make sure everything was alright."

"Yeah that makes sense," Sally interjected, "so I'm guessing you went? What did they say?"

"That's the thing. It hasn't been good news Sal. The doctor noticed I had some sort of pressure behind my eyes and she was apprehensive enough to send me to the hospital to see a neurologist," I noticed her eyes widening at that comment, "so we went to see the neurologist and he decided I needed to have a scan."

"What kind of scan?" Sally whispered, her eyes narrowing slightly as she realised I was about to tell her something serious.

"An MRI scan. I went for it yesterday. They found a mass on my brain which they suspect is a brain tumour. They took a sample of the tissue to find out what type of tumour I've got and what course of action needs to be taken."

Sally stared at me, her mouth dropping open in surprise. If it hadn't been such a hard thing to say to her, I most likely would have found her reaction comical and laughed. She floundered for a few moments, at a loss of what to say. In the end, her voice returned.

"You've got a brain tumour? What?! I never in a million years saw that one coming. Are you OK? How are you dealing with this?" she spewed out, firing the questions at me as they popped into her mind. I held my hand up to stop her from carrying on, hoping to calm her down slightly.

"I know it's a lot to take in, believe me. I think Cal's in shock but he's trying to be strong for me and I've not really taken it in and accepted it yet but a few days ago, my only issue was that I had to be pregnant for nine months. Now I've got this to deal with," I exhaled slowly, "I'm not going to get upset about it constantly because there's no point. I've already blarted on Cal's shoulder over it and although I'm not exactly happy about it, I'm not going to use my time up by thinking about all the different scenarios that can happen until I know exactly what I'm dealing with. There's simply no point."

Sally slumped back in her seat as though her body had just turned to jelly, unable to support her anymore. She gazed at me in what appeared to be amazement.

"That's a very positive way to look at things Amber. Good for you! How long do you have to wait for the results?" she questioned me.

"The doctor said that they should be back within the week," Cal piped up from his place in the kitchen doorway, "she's doing really well with the news isn't she? I'm waiting for her to realise how serious this is."

I could tell that he was trying to chide me by informing Sally about how I'd been over it but I ignored him. I knew I was perhaps being blasé over it all, but I'd always been a laidback type of person who didn't worry about problems until I knew what the problems were. I did not see the point in causing myself extra unnecessary stress, especially when I had another life growing inside of me. I rubbed at me stomach unconsciously, not noticing that Sally was watching my hand.

"How does it feel?" she asked gently. I gazed at her in curiosity, hoping she would elaborate on what she meant. Did she mean how did it feel that I'd been diagnosed with a tumour?

She nodded her head in the direction of my stomach, smiling.

"I mean, being pregnant. What's it like?"

"Oh! I did wonder what you were on about," I snickered at her, "it's...different. I don't know how to describe it. You know when you hear about women being attached to them and protective of them when they're pregnant, like even right at the beginning? That's true. Even though I've not met Little Bun yet, I feel like they're the most precious thing in this world. My protectiveness is in overdrive. Also, I'm feeling exhausted *all* the time! I've been informed that the first trimester is generally the worst one anyway and that once I'm into the second trimester, I'll start to feel better about it all and get this 'glow' that expectant mothers are supposed to have. We'll see, I'm not holding my breath."

"I hope you do feel better soon, from the pregnancy at least. When do you get to find out what you're having? And on that note, do you want to know?"

"Apparently we can find out at the mid pregnancy scan which is about sixteen weeks in. So I'm afraid we still won't know for a good while yet."

"Well, whatever you end up having, I know you'll be a great mum," Sally informed me in no uncertain terms, "and Cal will be a great dad. Promise me one thing though?"

"What?" both Cal and I asked in unison.

"Don't stop writing your steamy scenes in your books. We can't have you getting all tame on us! And Cal? You need to provide her with plenty of inspiration, understood?"

I burst out laughing as Cal grinned mischievously at us both.

"I understand completely Sally. Don't you worry, her inspiration is not about to run out any time soon, I can assure you of that."

He waggled his eyebrows at me suggestively so I threw the nearest cushion to me at his head, laughing the whole time.

"Cal!" I pretended to be scandalized, "you're not meant to encourage her you know!"

Sally was really fighting the laugh that was attempting to break free from her as she took in our exchange. She formed an innocent expression as she watched me.

"Who? Me? Don't worry hun, I don't need any encouragement. It's you that needs that so you can keep writing sexy novels for me to read!"

By that point, we were all laughing hard, and I knew that even though I was likely to have some dark days ahead, it was the moments like these that were going to get me through it. I currently had my fiancé and my best friend and my baby growing in my belly...things were as good as they could be. I intended to enjoy every single minute of it.

CHAPTER SEVENTEEN.

Four days after I'd had the scan and biopsy taken, I received the call from the hospital telling me that my results were back. They booked an appointment in for me to go and discuss the results with Dr Bradley the very next day and needless to say, I spent the rest of that day wondering what the results had been. Questions kept forming in my mind, running around and around my head. Why did I need to be seen so quickly again? What had they found? Was it something to worry about or was it a benign tumour that wasn't going to affect me much? If I needed treatment, what treatment would I need? Would I be allowed to have treatment whilst carrying a child in my womb?

I kept thinking of more and more things, until I forced myself to stop. I picked up the zodiac killer book to finish reading that, hoping I would be able to concentrate on that for a while and forget my own issues. It had turned out to be a good idea as I forgot about my own life for a time which helped me to relax. I'd got a headache once more, but due to the increasing amount of them that I had, I was able to carry on as I'd started to get used to them.

The following morning, Cal and I headed over to the hospital. We sat in silence as we drove, neither of us wanting to say anything as we pondered what was about to be told to us. We parked up in the car, walked in and checked in at the reception before sitting down to wait. Now I was feeling nervous. I'd been trying to stay positive about all of this, but not knowing was starting to get to me. If I just knew everything that I needed to, I would be alright. I was sure of it. We were only waiting for about ten minutes when my name was called.

Cal followed me into the room where we could see Dr Bradley sitting slouched at his computer, reading something on its' screen. When he heard us come in, he turned to face us with a grim expression upon his face. Alarm bells sounded in my head at the grave look he greeted me with. That couldn't mean this was going to go well. I gulped nervously. Panic thudded in my heart and I grabbed a hold of Cal's hand, holding on tightly as I prepared myself for the bad news that was surely about to come. We sat down silently in the chairs provided as we waited for the doctor to speak.

"Miss Ackles, thank you for coming in so promptly," Dr Bradley began, "we've had your test results back and I'm afraid to say that it is not good news for you."

Cal squeezed my hand whilst I tried to remain calm and composed. I didn't want to panic quite yet.

"What is it doc?" Cal asked anxiously.

"According to the tissue samples that we took during your biopsy and tested on, it has shown that you have a primary glioblastoma tumour."

I stared at him confused, not understanding what he was saying to me.

"What does that mean?" I prompted, hoping he would explain it in English to me. I wasn't a medical expert so telling me things using their technical terms was not a good idea because I didn't have a clue what he was talking about.

"A primary glioblastoma tumour is also known as an astrocytoma. It is an aggressive form of brain cancer which can be treated depending on the grade level it has progressed to. I'm afraid your case is extremely serious," Dr Bradley told me solemnly.

I took a minute to allow his words to sink in when I realised he hadn't told me something.

"What grade is my tumour at? Is it at a treatable level or am I in trouble?" I whispered, hoping against hope that it would be fixable. Dr Bradley's face soon extinguished that hope.

"The glioblastoma currently invading your personal space is a Grade 4. That is the highest level for cancer and in this case, with the type of tumour that you have, the survival rate is minimal," he paused briefly before carrying on, "it is still unknown to us what causes this type of tumour but what we do know is that once you start noticing the symptoms then it's already at a high stage. It is something that appears rapidly and there is most likely nothing that you could have done to prevent it."

I was gobsmacked. I slackened my hold on Cal's hand, noticing that he was staring at the doctor as though he didn't believe what he was hearing.

"When you say the survival rate is minimal, what do you mean? What am I looking at? Am I going to die?" I queried, not wanting to know the answers but I knew there was no way to avoid it. Dr Bradley looked stricken, as though he didn't want to answer my questions.

"We are able to offer you surgery to remove as much of the tumour as we possibly can but due to the type of tumour, it will be highly unlikely that we will be able to get all of it out. That said, if any is left, then it would grow back again just as quickly. It is not believed that you would be free of this tumour. We can however, offer you chemoradiation along with the drug Temozolomide to be taken after the surgery if you choose to take that option. This would help to reduce the tumour further and help to prolong your life."

It dawned on me with horrifying clarity what it was that he was telling me without actually saying the words. He didn't expect me to survive this. When a doctor said they could prolong your life instead of saying they could cure you, that was really all you needed to hear to know that you were going to die. I took a shaky breath in as I tried to wrap my head around this.

"Be honest with me Dr Bradley. When someone has this type of brain tumour, do they survive? If not, then what is the average survival rate? Please tell me the truth doc. I need to know."

"No. We don't have any records of other patients with this particular cancer surviving for more than five years. The average survival rate is in between twelve and eighteen months but it is possible that it could be less due to the fact that it is already at the end stage of the cancer by the time it comes to light. I'm sorry to tell you all of this Miss Ackles, truly I am but we shall work with you to make this as painless as possible for you."

Cal breathed in sharply. I looked over to see his face had gone white, just as it had the last time we were here, but this time I thought he might pass out. I squeezed his hand, trying to get him to come back to me, in the moment. His eyes were unfocused and unresponsive so I returned my attention to the doctor in front of me.

"We shall need to organise surgery for you soon so that we can try to remove what we can," Dr Bradley went on and I glared at him, starting to feel angry.

"What's the point?" I snapped. I didn't mean to take it out on him but I wasn't completely in control of my emotions anymore.

"Having the surgery will help to prolong your life. It means that you would live for longer," he replied unfazed. I realised that he must have to tell patients on a regular basis that they were dying and had probably seen many different reactions during his time there. I felt sorry for him as I knew it must be a hard thing to do but from my point of view, it was harder to hear it. I thought to myself for a few minutes.

"If I have the surgery, will it harm the baby? And on that note, am I going to survive this pregnancy?" I suddenly wanted to know what the implications of all of this were going to be.

"Whenever any surgery is performed on a female who is carrying a child within her, there are risks that the baby may be harmed, yes. There is the possibility that the foetus would not survive. In regards to surviving the pregnancy, then yes I believe you will get through it but that is my personal opinion and not a specific diagnosis so please do not take that as gospel," Dr Bradley insisted. I could tell that he was trying to give me a sliver of hope in the midst of all the angst that had arisen.

I felt completely floored. So I had been told that I was going to die but if I tried to prolong my life, then Little Bun might die? How was that fair? I knew one thing for certain, I was not about to lose my child because of this. I took a deep breath, uttering words that I'd never thought I would ever say.

"Am I likely to survive the pregnancy if I don't have the surgery?"

"No! You've got to have the surgery!" Cal cried in horror. I could see that he was struggling with the idea of losing me, but if this was what I needed to ensure at least one of us survived out of Little Bun and myself, then I was choosing Little Bun.

"No, Cal. You heard what Dr Bradley said. With or without the surgery, I'm going to die. Yes, I may live longer but it wouldn't be for very long and why would I risk us losing our child when we already know what the outcome is going to be for me?" I turned back to face the doctor calmly, "so back to my question, will I be likely to make it through and give birth to my child before I die?"

Dr Bradley nodded his head once.

"Yes," he replied, "there is a very strong possibility that you would survive to be able to give birth. But please be aware that there is a good chance that you might not survive too. At this point in time, there is no way of truly knowing what the outcome will be."

"But in order for my child to have a better chance of survival, it would be best if I avoided the surgery?" I pushed, wanting to know for certain. Dr Bradley sighed. I could see that he didn't want to give me straight answers but I was forcing his hand. I needed to know.

"Yes. I strongly recommend that you have the surgery Miss

Ackles but if you refuse, then yes, your child will have a much higher chance at surviving with no problems," came his defeated reply, "please be aware Miss Ackles, that your body will deteriorate much quicker than what you may anticipate. We will get you in touch with our care team so that we can provide you with the right amount of support and when you are close to your due date, there is a strong possibility that you will need to stay in the hospital so that we can monitor you and your condition, alright?"

I nodded my agreement, knowing there really wasn't anything else I could do. He wasn't happy with my decision I could tell but I think he knew where I was coming from when I made it which was why he wasn't trying to force my hand.

"Good," he said, "I'm going to give you some information to take home with you today so that you can have a read through it and help you to understand things easier. In the next few days, I would like you to think about what you want to do properly, to make sure that you truly don't want to have the surgery and that you've had time to decide that you are doing the best decision for the both of you ok? I would like you to let me know your definitive answer on what you wish to do by next week please. I know it's quick but time is of the essence. I'm just going to leave you for a couple of minutes whilst I go and fetch that information for you Miss Ackles. Please excuse me for a moment."

Dr Bradley rose from his chair and left the room swiftly, leaving Cal and I looking despondently at each other. What a crap day this had turned out to be. I fell back into my chair, resting my back against the chair as I tried to comprehend what had just happened during this meeting. I was dying. Me. Dying. I knew that it was going to take a long time for that to sink in. After all, who got used to the fact that they were dying with no hope of survival within a space of half an hour? Nobody, that's who!

"This sucks on a major level," I muttered, more to myself than Cal but he decided to reply regardless.

"That's an understatement. My choices here are to lose both you *and* the baby or lose you and *possibly* the baby! I can't believe this happening. I mean, what kind of a choice is that? I don't want to lose you and I don't want to lose our baby."

Cal scrubbed a hand over his face, the frustration etched into his very being. I felt for him, I did. We were supposed to be starting a life together, a family and that future had just been snatched away from us. I couldn't see how this was fair in any way.

"I'm sorry Cal," I mumbled, sadness threatening to overwhelm me. Cal's face crumpled at my words and he pulled me into a tight embrace, placing kisses on the top of my head as he held me close to him. He lowered his head and buried it into my neck, inhaling my scent. (I wasn't sure why he did that but he always had).

"It's not your fault, Amber. You couldn't have prevented this from occurring but I wish you'd talked to me first before refusing the surgery. I'd like to discuss it with you please, it's something that we *both* need to agree on. You're my fiancée after all."

I could hear the hurt in his voice at the fact that I hadn't consulted with him first and even though I understood that I perhaps should have discussed it with him before giving the doctor my answer, it made no difference. My answer wasn't going to change. I wanted Little Bun to live. I chose that this wasn't the time to argue with him however, so I placated him instead.

"You're right and I'm sorry that I didn't. It was a decision I thought you would agree with. You don't want to lose our child do you? You still want Little Bun even if I'm not around don't you?"

"Well of course I do," he retorted hotly, "Little Bun is a part of you! Thing is, I don't want you to not be a part of our lives anymore."

"I know babe. I don't want to leave you either but this is what we are being faced with. If you had the choice of losing both of us or the choice of being able to save one of us even though the other one would die, you'd want to save the one that you could wouldn't you?" I asked, trying to get him to see things from my view.

I could see the struggle on his face as he tried to come up with a feasible argument. It was interesting to watch the emotions as they ran across his features and I knew the exact moment when he knew that he couldn't give me a good reason for denial as his shoulders slumped down and he closed his eyes as he tried to calm himself. Opening his eyes again, he looked at me.

"You know I would," he muttered quietly, "I just wish I could save you both."

"Don't beat yourself up about it Cal. You can't do anything and it's enough to know that you would if you could. I love you and I know you love me. When Little Bun comes along, we shall both love him or her and after I'm gone, you'll have to give them our love for the both of us. I'm not going to lie to you Cal. I'm scared. This is the most frightening thing I can think of but I need to think about our baby as well. If I can leave one small part of me behind, then I'll always be with you. Every time you look at our child, you will be looking at half of you and half of me. Let's just hope they have my good looks eh?" I chuckled, attempting to lighten the mood slightly by making that joke.

He gave me a small smile in return.

"Yeah but maybe not your height. You're such a short arse," he laughed, returning a joke in my direction. At that moment, Dr Bradley strode back in with the information that he'd gone searching for. (I'd actually forgotten what we'd been waiting for whilst I was chatting with Cal, but that was just another symptom of this monster growing inside my head).

He handed the papers over to me, telling me that they explained all about glioblastomas and what I could expect in the coming months. He reminded me to call him by the following week with a decision that we'd both thought about and agreed upon before he allowed us to go. With a promise that someone would be in touch with me shortly to arrange a care/support team for me, we said our goodbyes and left.

I laced my fingers through Cal's as we strolled back to the car, enjoying the feel of the sunshine on my face. The sun rarely came out during the winter months so I appreciated this small amount that was warming my skin. I turned to Cal and gave him a kiss on the cheek before walking around to my side of the car and getting in. I knew I had his support. I knew that he would be there for me through the difficult times ahead.

CHAPTER EIGHTEEN.

Dearest readers,

I'm beginning to struggle with writing my story now. I shall keep writing for as long as I am able to but Cal will take over from me when I'm unable to continue.

So now you know what has been happening in my life. I must admit to you all, I am scared. I'd be lying if I said I wasn't but I'm also hoping that this book is giving you all a better insight to me and what I'm like.

In regards to whether I chose to have surgery or forego it to be able to have my baby, I chose to opt out of surgery. Cal and I had a long discussion about it and I managed to convince him that it would be the best option. I may not have met my child yet, but my love for them is strong and there was no way that I was going to risk losing them.

Cal has been taking exceptionally good care of me. On my bad days, he does everything I need him to but he doesn't mollycoddle me which I'm grateful for. I wouldn't want to be so it suits me well. I don't know what I would have done without Cal, he's been my rock.

Little Bun, I apologise for the steamy scenes you've read. I'm hoping that you've skipped over them if I'm honest but at the same time, if you have read them, at least you can see that mummy and daddy love each other very much. I'll always be with you Little Bun.

From Amber xx

*   *   *

The decision had been made.

I'd rang Dr Bradley after a couple of days to tell him what we'd decided. He checked with me yet again that I was sure about not going ahead with surgery or treatment to which I informed him that I was deadly certain. He told me that we would discuss options that would be available to me to support my decision until I was to meet my end. I'd hung up the phone, feeling awful after our conversation. It wasn't great listening to the doctor talk about your impending and unavoidable death.

Now all that we had left to do was to inform the family of what was happening. We'd managed to keep them all in the dark so far but now that I knew exactly what was wrong with me and what was (not) being done about it, it was time to tell them my fate. I called Ellen and Ryan whilst Cal called his parents, announcing that we were calling a family meeting and that everyone needed to attend our house the following day (it was a Saturday so nobody was working before you ask). Considering that family meetings were never ever called, everyone arrived at our house the next day with trepidation. You could see it on all of their faces that they knew that something was wrong. When you did something out of the ordinary though, it was always going to be obvious that there was something seriously wrong. I actually think we had freaked them out by calling this meeting. Go figure.

Ellen was the first to arrive, followed closely by Cal's parents and his brother as they'd came in the same car. We exchanged the usual pleasantries when we greeted each other, hugs and kisses being passed around between us like always. I asked them all if anyone wanted a drink. Ryan asked for a coffee which I promptly made for him but nobody else wanted anything so it didn't take me long to make.

As I handed Ryan his coffee, he frowned and stared at my hand.

"What's going on Amber? Your hand is shaking."

I didn't answer as I shook my hand to try and get myself to stop shaking. I knew we had to tell them about the fact that I was dying but I was scared to. This was going to be such a hard conversation to have and I wasn't one hundred percent ready to tell them yet, but as the doctor had pointed out to us at our appointment, time was of the essence.

I sat myself down on the floor cross legged in front of them all (as there were no more seats available) and Cal came and sat on the floor next to me, wanting to be by my side when I dropped this bombshell on everybody. He placed his hand at the small of my back, rubbing his thumb around in small circles to show me his support whilst not saying a word. I peered up at the family, all of them watching us curiously now as they waited for us to speak.

I took a breath to steady my nerves and began.

"We called all of you to come here for this family meeting because we've got something important to tell you. It's not good news I'm afraid so maybe brace yourselves a little."

Rachel gasped loudly, a hand fluttering to her throat.

"Oh no! Is it the baby? Have you lost it?" she cried in dismay, looking from Cal to me and back.

I shook my head with a slight smile, whilst Cal told his mum to be quiet and listen.

"No, it's not the baby," I replied, steeling myself against what I was about to tell them, "but the news we've got isn't any better. Do you all remember at Christmas when I kept getting headaches and I was sick so we came home early for me to get checked out by the doctor? Well, we went and asked the doctor if it was due to my being pregnant that I had been feeling unwell. It turned out that it wasn't. I've had to go and see a neurologist at the hospital and I've had an MRI scan and a biopsy done so that they could figure out what was going on."

I stopped, finding it difficult to carry on and glanced at Cal, wondering how I was going to continue. Thankfully, he stepped in then and took over with what I was saying.

"Amber went in and had the tests done which is when they discovered that she has a mass on her brain," I saw a tear glide down his cheek whilst he talked, "after we had the results back from the biopsy they did on her…they found…"

Cal trailed off, unable to say what he wanted to say at that moment as another tear leaked its way out of the corner of his eye.

"What? What did they find?" Ellen demanded, leaning forwards in her seat and gripping onto the arm of her chair with such strength that her knuckles had turned white.

"They found that I have got a Grade 4 brain tumour," I blurted out, not knowing how else I could say it. There were gasps and shocked faces around us now whilst I waited to allow them time to realise what I'd just said, "because of the severity of it, I have been informed that I'm not going to survive it. It's a very aggressive type of tumour that is apparently quite rare and even if I had surgery to try and reduce it, it would grow back so I would not survive for much longer either way."

Hot tears tracked down my face then. I couldn't hold it in any longer, I was so tired of trying to be brave. This was so unfair. I'd finally become a part of a family, gotten engaged and I was pregnant with Little Bun. Things had been looking really good for me and now, by some cruel twist of fate, I wasn't going to live to see any of it. I wasn't going to be able to grow old with Cal, I wouldn't see my child grow up. Hell, by the time they were taking their first steps and saying their first words, I probably wouldn't even be here anymore. How was that fair?

Ellen had tilted her head slightly, narrowing her eyes at me.

"What do you mean *if* you had surgery? Why is there an if in that sentence?" she asked, a frown pulling her lips down at the corners. I should have known that she would pick up on that. I gazed directly at her, holding myself steady.

"I mean, that I have chosen not to have surgery. I had a choice to make. Either I could have the surgery and risk losing the baby or I could not have surgery and ensure the baby would survive. I came to the conclusion that if I was going to die regardless, then why not try and save my baby?"

The room was completely silent. Harry was frowning whilst Rachel opened and shut her mouth like a fish in shock. Ryan's face had drained of colour (so he had the same reaction as Cal) and Ellen was staring at me in disbelief. Cal spoke up again then.

"We know this is a lot for you to take in so please take your time."

Ellen was the first person to speak up after that.

"Are you seriously going to let her do this?" she directed her accusing question at Cal. I threw a glare her way.

"This isn't something we've decided lightly, Ellen! And you can't blame Cal either. He wanted me to have the surgery but I convinced him otherwise. Put yourself in my shoes for a second. If you had been given the same choice as I have, what would you have done?"

Ellen paused at that, considering her answer. I kept talking.

"Let me put it to you this way," I said, "if you had just found out that you're going to die whether you had surgery or not and you were pregnant, the doctor's just told you that having surgery can put the baby's life at risk or you can give birth to the child relatively safely if you didn't have surgery, what choice would you make? What other choice could you possibly make? Kill your baby and die? Or save your baby and die? That's the choice I've been faced with and for me, it was an easy one to make."

I glared at her defiantly, silently daring her to question my actions again. I knew she was only concerned about me and that this was a huge shock to them all but did she honestly think I wouldn't have decided on the best course of action?

"You're right. I'm sorry sis," she mumbled, "I just can't believe what you're telling us. You're actually going to die?"

I nodded my head, my bottom lip wobbling as I tried to keep more tears at bay.

"How long have they said you've got?" Ryan asked quietly, earn-ing him a slap on the arm from his mother.

"How dare you ask her that?" she chided him crossly, swatting at his arm again as he tried to duck out of the way. I chuckled.

"Rachel, it's OK. He's only asking the same questions I did. We're looking at anything from twelve to eighteen months, probably less. I've been informed by the doctor that I should make it through the pregnancy but because I'm not having any treatment for the tumour, I probably won't last as long as the average person does who has this problem," I told them as if we were talking about something easy like the weather. I really didn't know how else I was supposed to say any of this so I spoke as I normally would. I let out a breath as I allowed them to take everything in in their own time. Cal's hand was wrapped around my shoulders now, leaning me into him in a supportive manner, knowing how difficult this was for me. I pressed a kiss against his cheek and snuggled up into the crook of his shoulder to show him how much I loved him without saying it. I knew that he was finding this just as difficult as I was but he was being a stalwart for me.

"We're so sorry Amber. What can we do?" Rachel asked gently. I smiled up at her from my position on the floor.

"There's not much anyone can do if I'm honest. My condition will deteriorate as time goes on and I'll probably need help eventually. I'd really appreciate it if you all could be there for Cal and help him through this too though."

"You don't need to worry about me, I'm not sick," Cal protested instantly.

"You may not be sick but you're going to watch me go downhill. When I'm gone, you're going to be raising our child on your own. You're going to need a lot of support in the future and I'd like to have it in place before I'm gone. I want to know that you're going to be OK," I told him, tearing up once more. Now that we were properly talking about things, I found I was feeling very emotional. I wanted to cry over everything.

Rachel patted me on my arm, returning my gaze to her kindly face.

"Don't you worry about Cal, my dear. We'll see to it that he has all the support he needs, I promise you that."

"Thankyou Rachel, I appreciate that. Can I also get you all to promise me something?" I asked, thinking I might as well ask what I wanted to whilst I was thinking about it.

"Sure, what do you want from us?" Ellen enquired.

"When Little Bun is old enough to understand, can you tell them about me? About their mum?" my voice faltered as I fought against the flood of tears that were trying to break through, "I'm not going to be able to see them grow up, but I want you to tell them how much I love them. I'd like you to tell them that as much as you can and if they ask any questions about me, I want you to answer them honestly so that they can know who I am. Or at least by the time they're asking, who I *was*."

The tears flowed then, cascading down my face as I burst out into sobs. I couldn't hold it in any longer. My heart was breaking as I thought about all of the things I was going to miss when I wasn't around anymore. Cal wrapped his arms around me tightly, whispering sweet things and kissing my head as I wailed in his arms. My shoulders heaved and shuddered as I was wracked by the sobs that had overtaken me. I cried and cried and cried, until I felt as though nothing was left, my breath still panting when the tears dried out and I came to a stop.

I scrubbed at my eyes miserably, not moving from Cal's embrace. He made me feel safe, albeit for a little while. Once I'd composed myself, I turned my tear streaked face towards the other family members, noticing that they all seemed awkward and sorrowed. I swallowed hard, trying to find my voice again.

"I'm sorry for that outburst," I apologised quietly, not wanting to look at any of them. Ellen came over to me and flung her arms around my neck, yanking me out of Cal's arms and into hers.

"You don't need to say sorry!" she cried, a few tears having leaked out of her own eyes, "It's understandable that you're upset! This is tragic news for you and I for one am going to miss you so so much. You're my sister and my best friend! I promise to you that we are going to help Cal in any way that we can because he is family now. We will help to look after Little Bun and we will tell them all about you and how amazing you are! Auntie Ellen is going to spoil him or her rotten ok?"

I pulled away to smile at her.

"Thankyou. I'm just scared of what's coming and I'm worried about Cal and Little Bun. I think I needed to make certain that they were going to have the support they will need. Silly of me to question it I know because I know all of you are going to help them without a doubt. I guess I just needed to hear it?"

I didn't think I was making much sense anymore but they all agreed with me so I think they understood what I'd meant. I cleared my throat, slapping my hands on my cheeks sharply to try and wake myself up out of my sadness.

"Being as you've all made it over, would you like to stay for lunch? You don't have to if you've got things to do but if you'd like to then you're more than welcome. We can talk about this business at another time now. Sorry if that sounds rude but I don't want to talk about it any more for today," I told them firmly, getting up from my position on the floor.

Harry clapped his hands together, making us all jump as he grabbed our attention.

"I think lunch sounds like a great idea! Can I give you a hand in the kitchen?" he asked, standing up from his seat and striding into the kitchen without waiting for me. I smiled at his disappearing back. If anybody was going to help us to act normal, it would be Harry. I followed him inside and together we made a variety of sandwiches for everybody with a large mixed salad bowl so that we had created a mini picnic of sorts. I gave Harry a kiss on his cheek as I turned to carry some of the food into the living room.

"Thankyou Harry. Thankyou for not treating me any different to usual."

CHAPTER NINETEEN.

After Cal's family and Ellen had gone home later that afternoon, I'd snuggled up on the sofa with Cal, resting against him as we watched a movie together. That had been nice. I can't remember the film itself that we had watched but I think it had been a romantic comedy. When it had finished, I turned to Cal and kissed him passionately, showing as much of my love for him as I could in that one kiss.

The kiss deepened, becoming more urgent until Cal groaned into my mouth. I smiled, thanking my lucky stars that he still fancied me after everything that had been going on and I climbed onto his lap.

"Oh babe, you're killing me," Cal moaned against my lips, "we can't do this in your condition."

"Why not?" I murmured into his mouth, grinding myself against him and placing his hands onto my breasts to let him know where I wanted him to hold me.

"You're pregnant and you know, the thing you didn't want to talk any more about."

"If we're gentle, we won't hurt the baby and the other thing isn't going to affect us tonight is it? Now shut up and kiss me. I've missed your touch."

I planted my mouth firmly onto his, grinding my hips against his as I helped him to massage my breasts. It wasn't long before I could feel his hard length straining against his trousers, poking at me through the material. I smiled, lowering my hands so that I could free him from his constraints. He groaned into my mouth as I took him into my hand, stroking his hard length whilst all the while keeping my lips on his, my tongue clashing with his inside our mouths. I felt him push my top up, over my head until it flew onto the floor as his gaze landed hungrily onto my bra. In the next instant, my bra had been unclasped and my breasts hung freely in front of him. He took one into his mouth as he used his hand to caress the other, whilst all the while I continued to stroke him.

"I think you need to lose something else," he growled into my ear, kissing along my neck before returning to lavish attention on my breast. I chuckled, arching my back as I spoke.

"If you'll take the time to see for yourself, you'll see there isn't anything in your way now."

He jerked back, his eyebrows raised in surprise. He lowered his free hand to reach under my skirt (yes I had chosen to wear a skirt that day. I did wear them on occasion) and I waited until he found what he was looking for. I gasped as he stroked against me, moving my hips against him more.

"Oh, when did you go commando?" he asked, "never mind. Tell me later. I want you now."

I giggled as he recaptured my mouth, positioning me over him until I was in the right place and then I slid down, his hard length stretching me deliciously. Yes, this is what I'd wanted. I'd wanted to know he still wanted me like this. I rose up and down, taking things slowly as we made love to each other, his hands constantly roaming over my body as he gently began to pick up the pace. He used those strong, masculine hands of his to help me bounce upon him faster and faster until I cried out. He roared out my name only minutes later, pulling me against him as he waited for the pulses to cease between us.

He stroked his fingers through my hair, tilting my head so that I could kiss him, the tenderness in the moment was something I'd been craving all day.

*   *   *

As the weeks passed, I found myself growing more and more tired each day as the headaches grew worse and my motor functions began to become harder to do. My stomach had grown in size too, the bump for Little Bun beginning to show a little more each day.

Cal had noticed that I was easily irritated these days with my emotions going from angry one minute to crying the next. Unfortunately, I didn't know if it was due to the pregnancy or the tumour. I began to feel sorry for Cal, apologising to him most days for my behaviour. I knew it must have been hard for him to deal with me but he was very sweet. He would kiss me each time and tell me that he loved me no matter what. It always melted me a little bit on the inside when I heard him say these things.

I'd also begun to receive regular visits from nurses and carers who wanted to check in with me to make sure that my condition hadn't deteriorated too much and to make sure that I was coping alright at home for the time being. I found those days harder than the rest because it was a constant reminder that my time was growing shorter with each passing day.

Ellen spoke to me every day, either on the phone or she'd come around to see me at the house. Harry and Rachel had also taken to coming around more often whilst Ryan checked in with Cal on how I was doing and how he was doing. I was pleased that everyone had rallied around us, especially so that Cal had other people to lean on too. When someone came to see me, I kept telling Cal to go out somewhere for some fresh air or to do something different because I knew he needed to have his space away from me. He'd always try to find a reason to stay with me of course, thinking he should stay but I insisted that he took the time for himself. I didn't want him to end up hating my existence during my last days on this earth as I think that would have broken me.

Eventually, the time came for my mid pregnancy scan. I was still able to get around alright, but Cal had to hold my arm most of the time to keep me steady as I was growing clumsier all the time. I looked it up to discover that that was actually a sign of my worsening condition due to the tumour but always tried to laugh it off to everyone else.

Sally sent me a text message on the day of the scan saying, *'Good luck for today! I think I'm just as excited as you are right now to find out if Little Bun is going to be a boy or a girl! Let me know as soon as you can xxx.'* I smiled at the message.

Unfortunately for my child, I had a distinct feeling that the nickname Little Bun would stick. If it was a girl it wouldn't be so bad but if it was a boy, I could imagine they wouldn't be too happy with their mummy over it. Oh well, sorry kiddo.

We set off for the hospital, this time heading towards the ward for expectant mothers. I bounced on my toes as we walked, excited to find out what our baby was growing to be. I could see Cal trying to hide his grin at my happiness, holding my hand as we checked in to be seen for the scan.

"What do you think Little Bun will be? A boy or girl?" I asked Cal, unable to hide my joy at finding out the gender of our baby.

"I have no idea," he replied, chuckling at me, "I'm happy with either. They're a part of you and that's all that matters to me."

"Aww, you always say the sweetest things," I told him, kissing him quickly on the mouth just as my name was called. I rolled my eyes at the interruption but stood up, Cal following me into the room.

The sonographer gestured to me to lay on the bed in the centre of the room and greeted us.

"How are you both today?" she asked kindly as she got her instruments ready.

"Good thank you," I replied, "we're both looking forward to finding out what we're having."

"Do you have a preference or are you happy with either?" the sonographer asked as she smoothed some cold gel over my tummy after getting me to lift my top up so that she could access my bump.

"We don't really mind. We've been calling the baby Little Bun for months now so it will just be nice to start trying to decide on their actual name," I laughed at the sonographers' expression.

"Little Bun is an unusual nickname, but it's nice," she said as her eyes moved to the screen when she placed the instrument onto my stomach that would allow us to see the image of our baby. She moved it around a little as Little Bun appeared on the screen, already appearing a lot larger than when we'd last caught a glimpse at the twelve week scan and I beamed up at Cal, watching as his own expression matched mine.

We both watched the screen intently, waiting for the woman to tell us the news. She looked back to us with a big smile upon her face.

"Congratulations! You're having a little girl!" she announced.

"A girl? Cal? Did you hear that? We're having a baby girl!" I cried happily, tears leaking out of my eyes as joy washed over me. Yes! I'd made it this far and we were having a girl!

"I'm so proud of you babe. You've carried our girl well," Cal murmured to me, unable to tear his eyes away from the image of Little Bun on the screen.

"She's also looking very healthy," the sonographer told us, grinning at our obvious joy. Thank God, I thought to myself, pleased to know that she was healthy and thriving inside my dying body. I'd wanted a little girl and I was getting one. I really hoped that I would be able to see her grow, even just a tiny little bit, before I left her in this world with her father.

I already knew that the second we left the hospital, we would be calling our family and friends to let them know that Little Bun was going to be a girl! Considering how awful I had been feeling recently, I was ecstatic to find out that Little Bun was healthy and happy on my inside.

*   *   *

Dear readers,

The time has finally arrived for me to hand this book over to Cal to complete for me. I am finding it too difficult to remember everything now. The tumour is slowly eating away at my brain, making every tiny thing so much harder than it needs to be.

This is my farewell to you all. I would like to say thankyou for following me through my writing career as well as through this horrible final journey of mine. I hope you have found my story interesting and have liked what you've read. I've always been a people pleaser and I like to make people happy. I truly hope that you have enjoyed getting to know me.

My fans throughout the years have been fantastic and I love you all.

Cal, I love you. Finish this story for the both of us and for Little Bun.

Little Bun, I love you and always will. I'm sorry I'm not there to see you grow up but I will be keeping an eye on you from wherever I may be.

Love always,

Amber xxx.

CHAPTER TWENTY.

To the readers,

It's Callum Jacobson here. I just wanted to write a quick note to you all in here as I've noticed that is what Amber was doing. Thank you for the support you have all shown to us through this trying time. I have not written anything for several months now. I don't even remember the last time I picked up a pen to write with other than signing forms etc, but I made a promise to Amber that I would finish this book for her so that Sally could publish it.

It will be hard to write but I'll stay true to what happened with Amber and our family. I made a promise that I intend to keep. So here goes.

Cal x.

*   *   *   **

As time passed, Amber grew steadily worse, her condition deteriorating at a faster pace.

Little Bun was growing well inside of my darling Amber's body, even as her mother grew weaker and weaker with each day that passed. Amber remained positive all the time, regardless of the fact that she was in obvious pain as the tumour began to grow more aggressive.

I supported her decision not to have the surgery for the sake of saving Little Bun but it was killing me inside to know that she was dying. The woman I loved was dying and I couldn't save her. I can't begin to describe to you how many sleepless nights I've had over that. It's in a man's nature to protect his loved ones but how could I protect her from something that I couldn't see? I felt angry for a long time. It wasn't fair. Why did the love of my life have to die? She was such a good person who deserved to live and there are so many people in this world that are bad who deserve to die instead of her. I know that's a horrible thing to say but it was how I felt. I simply couldn't understand it and I still don't.

I did my best to hide my emotions from Amber so that I could stay strong for her but she could always tell when I was struggling. It was as though she'd got a sixth sense when it came to me. I loved her for it, for how considerate she was. She was the one dealing with such an awful disease and yet, she was setting plans in motion to make sure that I would have people around me to help me and support me when she passed. She was my angel, the mother of my child.

There was one day in particular when she was in a lot of pain with the headaches that she kept getting. They were almost constant now, so much so that she'd gotten used to the smaller ones but when she had one of the bad ones, they would completely incapacitate her. Her memory was starting to falter more often too, one of the days she'd even forgotten about Sally! I don't think Sally was happy about that but she understood that Amber's condition was worsening. On the day I've mentioned, the pain became so bad for her that we had to rush her into the hospital.

The doctors came and pumped a bunch of medication into her to try and help ease her pain but they couldn't give her too much in case it harmed Little Bun. Amber had made it very clear to any doctor that she'd seen over the past few months that they weren't to harm Little Bun in any way, shape or form. Dr Bradley had gone in to see Amber then to assess her condition. When he came back out a short while later, he saw me and walked over.

"Mr Jacobson, it's good to see you although not under these circumstances. I assume that you can now tell that Amber's condition is reaching critical stages yes?" he asked bluntly, getting straight to the point. I nodded my head as I waited for him to continue. "I'm afraid she is going to need to stay in the hospital now so that we can monitor her on a daily basis. With the baby due in the next few weeks, it is her best option to stay in where we can look after her."

I reeled from this news. I'd known that she was getting worse, but she'd apparently gotten worse than I'd realised. I had a sneaky feeling that she'd been hiding things from me so as not to worry me. As much as I loved her for it, I wish I'd known because here we were now. Amber was officially being hospitalised. I discussed details with Dr Bradley who informed me that the next few weeks were going to be crucial. Without physically telling me, Dr Bradley implied that we were going to be lucky if Amber made it to the end of the pregnancy to be able to give birth. I didn't know what to say. What could I say? My Amber was dying and the end stages were upon us. I can't describe to you how I felt in that moment so I'm not going to try.

I remember calling my family, Ellen and Sally to let them know where we were and what Dr Bradley had just told me. We were now running out of time and I needed them there. Once I'd finished the phone calls, I went into the room where Amber lay on the bed, her eyes closed as she slept peacefully. I sat down in the chair beside her and took her hand in mine. I was in shock. How long did I have left with her? Would we get a chance to see Little Bun or would we be too late? I knew that Amber would hold on, fighting to ensure our baby's safety but I wasn't sure what was happening to her now.

I held her hand in both of mine, resting my forehead against them. I don't know how long I stayed in that position but my mum touched my arm when she arrived, letting me know that she was there. I smiled thinly at her.

"Thanks for coming mum," I said as I gave her a hug. My dad was standing just inside the doorway whilst Ryan stood next to him. They both shook my hand, asking how she was doing.

I motioned for them all to follow me outside. I didn't want to be in the middle of talking to them when Amber woke up to hear something that she wouldn't want to know. Facing them, I took a breath to speak but heard footsteps running up behind me.

"Cal! How is she? What's happening?" Ellen gushed, panting a little to indicate that she'd ran from the carpark.

"You're just in time. I was about to tell my family so this makes it easier to tell you all at the same time," I paused briefly, "Dr Bradley has admitted her like I told you all on the phone. He's told me that she's getting worse and that her time is running out. At the rate she's deteriorating, he's concerned that she may not survive the pregnancy. If that is the case, then they're going to ask Amber's consent to perform a caesarean to get Little Bun out whilst she's still alive. I honestly don't know what to do here guys, my world is in there and it's falling apart."

I felt my face crumpling as the tears came spilling out of the corners of my eyes. I couldn't stop them. I didn't want to. It was better to get them out now whilst Amber was still asleep. That way, I could be strong when I spoke to her about it all when she woke up.

Mum wrapped her arms around me, allowing me to cry into her shoulder until I'd composed myself. I was falling to pieces. Amber was my other half, my soulmate. I didn't want to lose her.

"We're here for you honey," Mum soothed me, looking into my eyes now that I'd quieted down.

"I know and thankyou. I appreciate it. I'm sorry for this news Ellen. I know this must be just as hard for you."

Ellen's eyes were downcast as she spoke to me.

"I just want to be here with her. I appreciate you calling me and allowing me to be a part of her final weeks."

We continued our discussion for a while longer until I checked in on Amber to find that she'd woken up. She had appeared confused as to why she was in the hospital. I'd realised that she didn't remember getting there or why. I gently broke the news to her of what Dr Bradley had said to me. The horror that flashed across her face mirrored the agony that I was feeling on the inside. When I explained that there was a possibility that she may need to have a caesarean to be able to give birth to Little Bun, she didn't even flinch. Instead, she asked me if I could find Dr Bradley so that she could book a caesarean in to be on the safe side.

I did as she asked but now I was worried. Her reaction hadn't been what I'd expected it to be. She'd kept a straight face for the most part and spoken to me in a calm manner which concerned me. I wasn't entirely certain that what I'd said had truly registered with her.

*   *   *

A couple more weeks had passed.

Amber continued to decline during that time so Dr Bradley booked the caesarean for as soon as possible. Luckily, there was only a few more weeks before the baby was due so even though she would be premature, it wouldn't be by too much. Ellen had gone to the hospital every day around her job, relieving me to go and have a shower and some food for a short time before I would go back to be by Amber's side. During those first few days that she'd been in the hospital, Amber told me about this book and what she wanted me to do with it. We'd discussed many things but in the last day or so, I'd noticed that the conversation was getting harder to maintain, that she was starting to struggle with even the simpler things. It was hard to witness but I wasn't about to leave her side. She needed to know that I was there for her, through thick or thin.

When the day of the caesarean arrived, I was awash with nerves. Ellen, my mum and Sally all came to see Amber before she went in for the procedure and then they waited with me whilst the caesarean took place. I paced about the waiting room, unable to sit still. I was scared of losing Amber in there and possibly even Little Bun. I couldn't rest until I knew that they were safe.

Eventually, one of the doctors came out to me.

"Would you like to meet your daughter?" he asked smiling brightly at me.

I nodded my head in a daze. I was going to meet Little Bun! Which meant that she was alright. I followed the doctor back into the room, looking at Amber as she held our baby girl in her arms, smiling down at her. I strode over to her side and kissed her on the head, before taking a good look at Little Bun. She was perfect. Tiny and perfect.

I couldn't believe it. My daughter had been born into the world at last. I crouched down next to them both, smiling at Amber.

"You did good mummy," I reassured her, taking Little Bun's hand in my own. Technically, I gave her my finger which she curled her hand around but it was still adorable. Amber watched me as I met my daughter.

"We both did good daddy," she murmured to me. It was her. That was my Amber staring back at me. It was rare that I saw her like this these days. I was overcome with joy, tears springing to my eyes as I kissed her on the mouth.

"I love you, Cal. I'm sorry about everything you've been going through. Truly I am," she whispered, tears filling her eyes. I hated to see her upset but I knew it was because she could remember what was happening.

"Ssh babe, it's OK. Let's just enjoy this moment. You're here, Little Bun is here and this is perfect. I love you so much."

I saw her gaze back down at our bundle of joy in her arms, cuddling Little Bun close against her body. Amber glanced back up at me in a swift motion.

"What are we going to call her?" she asked, pursing her lips.

"I don't know," I replied, "what does she look like to you?"

"Hmm. To me she looks like a Lily. What do you think?"

I gazed down at Little Bun, rolling the name Lily around on my tongue for a minute. Yes, I liked it. Lily like a beautiful little flower. I smiled back at Amber.

"Yeah I like it. Lily it is."

Amber grinned back at me, placing her hand over the one holding mine and Little Bun's. I saw a bright flash. Turning around, I saw Ellen standing behind me with her phone in her hand. She'd taken a picture of us.

"Sorry if I made you both jump," she apologised, "but that was such a cute little family moment that I had to take a picture. Can I take some more?"

"Sure, go ahead," I told her, a smile playing upon my lips. I wasn't about to stop her taking photos of my beautiful little family. I didn't know how many I was going to be able to get of this time together and I wanted as many as possible.

My mum and Sally came into the room after a short time because they wanted to meet Little Bun and see how Amber was doing. I could see the delight on their faces when they noticed that Amber was functioning fully as though there was nothing wrong with her. The happiness in the air was palpable at that. It was turning out to be one of the best days we'd had in a while, where we had our Amber back.

(Readers, I am aware that I haven't described in detail how bad Amber got during the course of this illness but there are two reasons for that. One: I can't write it. Maybe, many years in the future I might be able to but right now and for a long time to come, I just can't do it because it hurts too much. Two: I don't want to upset Lily, also known as Little Bun, when she grows up to read this. When she's old enough and if she wants to know, I'll tell her then but until that time, I'm keeping it with me. Sorry).

I took a few photos myself by using my phone and I instructed

Sally and my mum to both take as many photos as they could. I know it probably appeared like overkill with taking pictures but again, I wanted as many as possible from now on so that I could show them to Little Bun when she was older. Pictures of her in her mummy's arms and also with the three of us altogether as a family. I couldn't ask for more right then.

Mum and Sally stayed with us for a couple of hours but eventually left to give me and Ellen time with Amber and Little Bun. We chatted to her, laughing about different things and all taking turns to hold Little Bun. Amber was animated as she spoke with us, telling us about various things that she'd like for us to do with Little Bun in the future that she wouldn't be able to. Things such as, Ellen had to take her shopping and for girlie days whilst I had to lead her down the writing path, encouraging her to read and to write on a regular basis. I think Amber secretly wanted our daughter to be like us.

The time passed quickly and evening came. It was about nine o'clock at night when Amber began to fall asleep on us.

"Cal? I'm so tired. If I fall asleep on you, I'm sorry," she murmured, yawning as she spoke.

"That's alright babe. You can sleep if you want to. You must be exhausted from today and meeting Little Bun at last," I told her gently, "go to sleep if you need to."

She glanced over at Ellen then.

"Ellen? Thanks for sharing this with us today. I'm glad you've been here. Can you make sure that Cal gets some rest?" she asked quietly, her eyes beginning to close although she was fighting to stay awake.

"Yes, of course I will. I'll leave you both to say goodnight whilst I wait outside. Goodnight sis. Love you," Ellen told her, putting an arm around her shoulder to give her a quick hug before leaving the room.

"The nurse is going to come and kick you out soon, you know,"

Amber joked as she turned back to me. Unfortunately, it wasn't too much of a joke because I really did get kicked out at night by the nurses now because otherwise they knew I wouldn't go home or get much sleep. I knew they did it for my own good but I always wanted to stay by my fiancée's side. I could never see what was wrong with that.

"Yeah I know," I chuckled at her, my gaze softening as I watched her for a minute, "I love you Amber. So much. I can't thank you enough for bringing Little Bun into the world. I promise I'll look after her but we're going to take as many photographs as possible of her with you so that we can show them to her when she's older. I promise you that she will know her mum."

Tears brimmed at the bottom of Amber's eyes, holding themselves there as she fought to keep herself from crying.

"Thank you," she said at last, her voice breaking, "I'm glad…and I'm scared, Cal. I'm really scared."

I took a hold of her hand and brought it up to my mouth so that I could kiss her on her knuckles. I hated to see her hurting like that, especially when I couldn't make things better.

"I know you are babe. I'm scared too. I can't imagine my life without you in it," I told her, my throat clogging up all of a sudden, "all I can say is that I love you with all of my heart and I always will. You're mine and I'm yours."

The tears that had been threatening to fall finally did so, streaking a wet trail down her cheeks as she gazed at me lovingly.

"I love you too Cal. I've been blessed to have you in my life. I love you so much! You and Little Bun," she cried, pulling me against her for a cuddle and a kiss, "now go home and get some rest before we both turn into a blubbering mess. I'll go to sleep and when I wake up, I'll see you in the morning alright?"

I studied her for a beat before replying.

"Alright. You rest up good and I'll see you and Little Bun first thing in the morning. I love you babe," I told her again, kissing her fully on the mouth.

"I love you too," came her reply against my lips as she returned my kiss tenderly.

CHAPTER TWENTY ONE.

It was 3am in the morning when my phone ringing woke me up.

I'd gone to bed happy, thinking about Amber and Little Bun as I'd fallen into a deep slumber. The phone ringing took a short time to register but as soon as I realised what it was, I sprang up to answer it. The only people who would be calling me in the middle of the night would be the hospital. I grabbed my phone up and hit the button to answer the call to see who it was. It was indeed the hospital.

"Mr Jacobson? I'm sorry to call you but you need to get here right away. Amber is deteriorating and you need to get here," the woman on the end of the phone spoke urgently.

I could tell from her tone that this was it. This was the moment I had been dreading. I told her I was on my way, already throwing my clothes on as I made my way down the stairs and out of the door. As I raced over to the hospital, I rang Ellen and my mum to tell them to get to the hospital. Now. I threw my car into park and ran inside the building, heading straight up to Amber's room to be greeted by doctors and nurses all crowded into the room, some of them starting to come away.

The sight filled me with dread. Why were they walking away? I ran up to them, pushing my way into the room to see Amber laying there, seemingly asleep.

"What's happened?" I demanded, turning to Dr Bradley who was stood there. He appeared grey in the face, whilst exhaustion was plain to see. I briefly wondered how many hours he'd been working for that day until he spoke to me gently, pulling me over to the side by my arm.

"Mr Jacobson, I'm so sorry," he began, "we did all that we could but I'm afraid I have to inform you that Miss Ackles has passed away."

Cold prickled its way all along my skin as I felt as though I'd been punched in the stomach by this news. I was reeling.

"What happened? You're telling me she's dead? She was great when I left here a few hours ago!" I cried, my voice rising with each word that I spoke. I couldn't help myself. He was telling me that the love of my life was gone. Dr Bradley sighed sadly.

"I'm sorry Mr Jacobson," he tried again, "yes, she did seem to be doing much better yesterday but as we have made you aware, her condition has worsened tremendously over the past several weeks. When the nurse called you, it had been noticed that Miss Ackles was having trouble with her breathing. We tried to help her but there was nothing we could do. I'm afraid she's gone."

He indicated to the other people in the room to leave as I stared at him, uncomprehending. She was dead. My Amber was dead. Dr Bradley placed a hand on my arm as he continued speaking.

"I'm truly sorry for your loss. She was a lovely woman. We have taken your daughter to be monitored by the nurses on the maternity ward for now, until you are ready to see her so please don't worry as we shall take good care of her for you. I'm going to leave you to have some time to yourself. Again, I'm very sorry."

And with that, he was gone. That was when I noticed it. The silence. The room was completely and utterly silent. I looked at Amber lying on the bed and tried to swallow the lump in my throat. She seemed so peaceful as though she were just asleep but I knew it wasn't true. I could see for myself that she wasn't breathing. Her chest was still, the sounds of her breathing no longer filling the room.

I went over to her, touching her hand with my finger. She was still warm. I sank into the chair by the side of the bed, taking her hand in my own as I tried to hold onto her even though she had gone. She had seemed so much like herself that I'd thought we'd gotten a bit more time together. I understood now that it had been the calm before the storm. She'd perked up for a time before her body gave up on itself. I couldn't believe it.

That was when I broke down, sobbing my heart out at the loss of my angel.

*   *   *

The day of the funeral came.

We'd had to arrange it of course and I'd had help from my mum and from Amber's sister, Ellen. Dad and Ryan had helped too because I found it hard to function with the knowledge that Amber was gone. The only thing keeping me going at that point was Little Bun.

She was absolutely gorgeous, my perfect little girl. I'd been able to bring her home with me fairly quickly and I'd been trying to adjust to life with looking after her. Naturally, my mum and Ellen came around every day to give me a break and to show me various things that might help. Amber and I had already bought everything we'd needed for when Little Bun was born so that was something.

As we walked into the church on the day of the funeral, I followed the coffin in as I carried our baby girl. Little Bun was fast asleep at that point so I was hoping that we would get through before she woke up and began crying. She always woke up crying. I'd realised pretty quickly that it was because she appeared to always be hungry because as soon as she was fed, she'd stop and hold onto me with her tiny little fingers.

There was so much of Amber that I could see in her whenever I looked at her and it hurt. I love Little Bun to bits, please don't get me wrong, but it hurt that her mother wasn't there with us.

The funeral itself was nice. I never know how else to describe a funeral but it went well which was a relief. We said the prayers, we sang the hymns, and we listened to the music. When it came to having Amber's coffin lowered into the ground, we went outside to the graveyard where we laid her to rest. I was in pieces by the time we reached that part of the funeral. I still hadn't come to terms with the fact that she was gone. I know we'd been expecting it and we'd known that this was how things would end up, but nothing can truly prepare you for death. For losing someone you've loved, lived your life with, and made future plans with.

At the very start of the year, we had been planning to get married and start our family with Little Bun. Before we had known about Amber's diagnosis, we had talked about things we'd wanted to do. Places we would go on holiday, day trips we would go on with Little Bun and general toys we would buy for her. We had even spoken about what our lives would be like in the future, whether we would want more children and if we would still fancy each other when we were old and grey. Now, I was burying the mother of my child, facing a future without her in it.

We held the wake at a local pub where there was a huge spread of food and the place was packed out with people wishing me their condolences. I'd known Amber was popular but seeing all of these people coming to pay their respects to her, I was overwhelmed.

I kept a hold of Little Bun throughout that whole day as I didn't want to part with her. It seems silly when I think about it, but she's the last piece I've got of my Amber.

Months passed by.

I slowly began to get used to my life as it was now. I took care of my daughter whilst adjusting to life without Amber and on occasion, I found glimmers of happiness starting to reappear in my life. These were always when Little Bun was being extra cute or she did something for the first time. My daughter was such a bundle of joy that my heart would melt when she gave me her adorable little smiles.

Then one day, I pulled out this book. I took a deep breath and began to read what Amber had written down. I must admit that I was surprised that she told you all the very intimate details of our love life but I decided to keep them in because she'd written those words. This is her book and I'd promised her that I would finish it.

So after I'd read through it all, (having a good cry whilst I did so), I picked up my pen and began to write. I wanted to finish what she'd started. I had made her the promise that I would and I had full intentions to stick to my word.

After I finished it, I called Sally. She'd come around that very day to see me and to collect the copy of the manuscript that I'd prepared for her. She'd gone away to read it, only to call me within two days of leaving in tears. She had already agreed to publish it with Amber when Amber had asked her to but she hadn't realised how honest and raw it would be.

We set about getting it published, choosing a book cover and making sure that it was exactly how we wanted it to be. And now, here we are. You have the book in your hands.

Epilogue.

Dear readers,

Thank you for purchasing this book. I believe Amber would have been very proud to see people reading about her story. I still don't know how well received this book will be but I have had many of Amber's fans informing me that they would like to read it so that they can get to know her better.

I thank Amber every single day for bringing our daughter into this world. If it wasn't for Little Bun, I don't know how I would have survived these past few months. I miss her like crazy and the only thing that brings me any peace about the whole thing is knowing that she's no longer suffering.

So to her fans, I hope you enjoy what you have read here.

To Little Bun, your mum loves you and she is watching over you from above.

Thankyou all for your support throughout what has been the most difficult time of my life.

From Cal x.

Printed in Great Britain
by Amazon